LONE WOLF'S CLAIM

THE KINCAID WEREWOLVES ONE

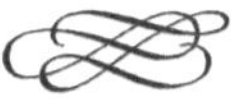

L.E. WILSON

EVERBLOOD
PUBLISHING

le@lewilsonauthor.com

Print Edition

Publication Date: May 24, 2016

ISBN: 978-1-945499-46-3

DEDICATION

To my readers.
You are awesome.
Thank you.

CHAPTER 1

The hunt was on.

Brock lifted his face to the cool evening breeze and took a deep breath through his nose. The faint, musky scent of Scottish heather blossoms lingered in the air and tickled his senses.

A strange thing to be smelling in the middle of downtown Seattle, he had to admit.

His sapphire blue eyes sparkled with anticipation. He was getting close now. Another few minutes and he'd be watching the seductive sway of Heather's full hips as she sashayed down the city street.

The thought made his mouth water and the blood pulse heavy within his veins.

Another waft of scented air hit him straight in the groin. In response, a feral growl rumbled up from his chest, and he picked up his pace. Head and shoulders taller than any of the human stragglers that were still out this late, he received more than a few sideways looks as he plowed down the sidewalk.

Inhaling deeply for more of the sweet scent, he moaned aloud. He could practically taste her. Heather Knight: the human female with eyes the color of a fine cognac, warm chestnut hair, and thick, womanly curves he couldn't wait to get his paws on.

He'd met her only a few hours ago, after following her friend to an apartment building. She'd opened her door dressed in nothing but yoga pants and a tank top, every curve on full display, and he'd been wrapped up in knots over the woman ever since.

And now she was running from him. Running from a *werewolf*.

A predatory smile lit his eyes.

Silly girl.

hit, shit, shit.

Heather looked back over her shoulder as she hurried to get across the street before the light turned green. Not that there was much traffic this time of the night, but with her luck, she'd manage to walk right in front of the one and only car that *was* on the road.

By some miracle, she made it safely to the other side, and then promptly tripped up the curb and onto the sidewalk, barely catching herself before she face-planted on the dirty concrete.

Seriously?

Pulling her blue, borrowed, running jacket back into place, she kept going as if nothing had happened, grateful that there wasn't anyone around at the moment to witness her near fall. It's not like she was one of those tiny girls that could get away with being klutzy and people (aka - guys) just thought it was cute. Nooo. She was twenty-eight, not quite five foot nine, and…

Well, let's not go there. Suffice it to say, she was definitely not in any danger of ever being accused of starving herself.

Heather jerked at a loud clank behind her, her heart leaping wildly within her chest, but it was just a construction truck finishing up some roadwork before the early morning rush hour. She admonished herself for being so jumpy, but she had the strangest feeling that she was being followed.

A certain tall, dark, and handsome picture of manly yumminess flitted through her mind, and she glanced behind her again, managing *not* to trip this time.

He wouldn't.

Would he?

She shook her head and pushed down the tiny piece of hope that was trying to float to the surface of her despair. Brock Hume would not be following her. Why would he?

Yeah, yeah, so they'd exchanged some flirty looks and maybe, possibly, she had made an innuendo or two (or four) on the flight here from their home in China. That didn't mean he'd go through all the trouble of following her when she left. That man was—

Nice? Tall? Brave?

Nope, there was just no other way to put it. He was hot, sticky, sex on a stick was what he was. He could get any woman he wanted.

A prettier woman.

A skinnier woman.

A woman who didn't know, or didn't care, that he wasn't a man at all, but a freaking werewolf.

Remembering her shock when she'd found out upon

their arrival in Seattle that he howls at the full moon once a month, she wondered how she hadn't figured it out earlier. No mortal human was that hot. The guy had to be at least six-foot-seven of pure muscle. Long brown hair, shot through with gold highlights, hung thick and wavy past his shoulders. Bright blue eyes had smiled at her from underneath heavy, dark brows and a wide forehead. And a trimmed beard did nothing to hide his strong jaw and perfect lips.

Heather heaved a wistful sigh.

But it was more than his good looks. And she—of all people—should have sensed it right away. Yet, she hadn't. Not in the slightest. And that was what worried her more than anything.

Turning the corner, she saw the stop ahead where she could catch the light rail back to the airport. She checked her phone for the time. It was almost four in the morning, and the next train didn't come for another forty minutes. She could try to call a cab, or she could just wait.

Glancing around, she saw the usual suspects hanging around on the street: a group of late night partiers stumbling home from the bar, shouting obscene words every few steps at no one in particular. A middle-aged couple waiting at the stop with their suitcases, shaking their heads and tsk'ing at the young people. And a couple of homeless guys talking quietly on the corner. Safe enough.

As she passed them, she did what she always did when she came across someone who was down on their luck. She fished out a couple of twenties and pressed one into each of their hands. "Get something to eat with this, ok?"

After a surprised pause, the older one told her, "Yes,

ma'am. Thank you. Thank you. God bless you." His hair was white as snow against his dark brown skin, and his black eyes were tired, but kind. They crinkled at the corners when his face lit up in a grateful smile.

She smiled back at him and started walking again. "Food. I mean it."

"Yes, ma'am," he called after her.

She arrived at her stop and smiled at the middle-aged couple, then pulled out her cell to call her parents back in Dalian. As she listened to their phone ring on the other end of the line, she mentally figured out the time difference. It was the evening of the following day at her parent's house, and they were probably getting ready for bed.

"Hello? Heather?" her mom answered right before voice mail picked up.

"Hi, Mom."

"Where are you, honey? I thought you were coming over for dinner tonight? Did you have to work late at the hospital again?"

"No. I've got a couple of days off, believe it or not. I'm actually in Seattle right now."

"Seattle? As in Seattle, Washington?"

"That would be the one. Long story, Mom. I'll catch you up when I get home."

The silence on the other end of the phone was deafening.

"Mom?" she asked. "Are you there?"

"Heather, get out of that city right now."

Heather frowned. She'd never experienced that particular tone in her mom's voice before. Granted, she'd never been a problem child, but she'd heard her fair share of tones from her mother's mouth all the same. And *that* was not one of them.

She heard her father asking what was going on and her mom answering him, speaking fast and quiet. He didn't sound happy either. Confused but not wanting them to worry, she hurried to reassure them. "Well, I'm actually at a stop right now waiting for the light rail to take me to the airport so I can fly home."

"Heather," her mom said. "Listen to me very carefully. Do not wait for the light rail. You need to get into a cab. Right now. Do you hear me? Find a cab, and get to the airport."

She looked up and down the street. Yeah, not many cabs cruising around at 4AM. "Mom, it's after four in the morning here…"

"Go, Heather! Now! Steal a damn car if you have to! Get on a plane, and take the first flight out of there to anywhere else. Then call me and let me know where you are and we'll get you home."

"All right, all right." She looked around again. Still no cabs, or cars to hijack for that matter. "Are you going to tell me what this is all about, Mom?"

"I'll tell you when you get home. Just get the *hell* out of there. And hurry! Before they find you."

The shock of hearing her mother actually curse ringing in her ear, Heather agreed without any more questions or arguments. She hung up the call.

What in the world was that all about? Who was going to find her? She thought about calling her friend Grace (after all, she was the reason Heather was in Seattle to begin with), but then remembered Gracie had lost her cell phone and hadn't gotten a new one yet. Besides, the chances were good that her best friend was busy with her sexy British boyfriend. At least she hoped she was. They'd flown all the way from China to get to his friends in the off-chance they could help him. Hopefully, he'd shown up here by now too. Gracie deserved some good stuff in her life.

Heather glanced around the interior of the rain cover she was under, looking for taxi advertisements, as she wasn't familiar with this city. When she didn't see any, she thought about asking the middle-aged couple if they knew the names of any so she could look it up, however they were huddled together in the corner, arguing about whether they should have taken a shuttle or not.

Pulling up her browser on her phone, she tried to Google it, but her signal was low and it was taking f-o-r-e-v-e-r. So she finally decided to just start walking back toward the apartments where Gracie was staying. If she didn't see a taxi on the way, she'd see if Grace or someone else there could give her a ride. Hopefully she could get in and out of the building without running into a certain werewolf—the reason she was leaving to begin with—as he was staying there too.

As she passed the homeless guys again, the younger one stepped toward her. "Where are you going?"

Still worried about how her mom had acted on the phone, she glanced over distractedly as she walked by. "Oh, change of plans. You guys take care."

He reached out and grabbed her arm before she could

walk away. "I don't think you understand. Where are you going? Heather? Is that what it is now?"

Well. *That* got her attention.

She took a closer look at him. He didn't look familiar. Frowning, she was about to tell him he must have mistaken her for someone else when the wind picked up and his dirty blonde hair blew away from his eyes. As she watched in disbelief, the irises swelled and contracted and changed until she was looking into a kaleidoscope of colors radiating out from the pupils.

Tearing her eyes from the hypnotizing display, she looked at his ears. His skullcap covered them, but she could see the distinct outline of a pointy tip on the one side.

No, it couldn't be.

Mind-numbing fear began to slide its icy fingers through her veins as it all suddenly became perfectly clear. She wanted to run away but she couldn't move, couldn't speak, as her eyes were pulled back to his without her control.

"Hey, man," the older man came to her rescue. "Leave the nice lady be now. She's been nothing but kind to us." When the other man ignored him and refused to release her, he pulled the twenty she'd given him out of his pocket. "Here, man. Here. You can have my part of the money that she gave us."

Not taking his strange eyes from her, he responded, "I don't want your money, old man."

She took a fortifying breath and forced herself to smile at the old man's concern. "It's okay. We know each other. This is my long, lost…cousin. Uh, Frank. Yeah. I just didn't recognize him before. We haven't seen each other in a long time."

Her rescuer glanced back and forth between them, seemingly unconvinced.

"Really," she assured him. "It's okay. We just have some family stuff to hash out. You know how that is. I'll be perfectly fine. I promise."

As she watched, the younger guy's eyes glimmered once with approval, and then faded to a muddy brown again. Still not releasing her arm, he turned to grin at his friend. "It's all good, Ed. Thank you for helping me out last night. I didn't realize Heather lived here. I'm just surprised to see her is all. Go on and get yourself a good breakfast, and maybe I'll catch up with you in a bit."

The old man still didn't look completely convinced, but as they were both standing there smiling their assurances at him, he muttered, "Sure, ok. I'm just gonna head right over to the convenient store there. Get a few things. I'll be back in a few minutes." With one last wary look, he ambled off to spend his money.

Heather ripped her arm from his grasp. "Who the hell are you?" she demanded, her voice sharp. Now that her fear was fading, her natural feistiness made a swift comeback.

"Don't be coy," he told her. "You know who I am. Or at least *what* I am."

He was right. She did. "What do you want with me, Frank?" she asked.

He gritted his teeth at the made-up name, but only said, "We'll let the prince decide that."

"The prince?" The freaking prince was here in Washington? No wonder her mom had nearly lost it when she'd found out where she was. Of course, they could've warned her not to come here. You know, any time during the last twenty-eight years or so.

He ran his eyes up and down her body. "Look at you! All grown up now. I almost didn't recognize you. How are the folks? You know, the ones that have been hiding you from your own people."

Taking her by the arm again without waiting for her to respond, he pulled her toward the tracks. "Come on, I hear our ride coming."

Heather dug in her heels, attempting to stay where she was without making too much of a scene. She didn't want to endanger the few humans in the area. "Just hold on. Where are we going?"

"I told you. To the prince." He tugged her along easily in spite of her best efforts to keep them where they were, in plain sight of witnesses. His slight form easily disguised how strong he really was.

Heather started to panic. This was bad. This was really bad. Her parents had spent the past twenty years of their lives hiding her from their kind. What were the odds that one would find her here, in Seattle? And at this particular stop? At four o'clock in the morning?

The only reason she was in this city at all was because Gracie and her boyfriend had gotten themselves into some trouble with some thugs back home in China. They'd gotten separated, and Grace had given her captors the slip and shown up at Heather's apartment. She'd needed to get out of the city, and Heather had invited herself along.

Brock knocking on her door shortly after Grace had arrived and joining their party was not why she'd come with them. It wasn't. For real. She would've kept her friend company anyway. Having that hunk of a man to look at (and to keep her warm on the plane) had just been a bonus. The fact that he had saved them both from a certain grisly death helped also. Those thugs had found their way to her apartment. And if she had stayed, it would not have been pretty.

And yeah yeah, she had promised Gracie she'd stay away from him, and she had kept her promise...sort of... even though she hadn't understood what her friend was all in a tizzy about at the time. Now she knew it was because Grace had found out, somehow, that he's a were-wolf. And when Heather was told that little piece of information? Yeah, she'd agreed with Grace. She needed to stay away from him. Hence the reason she was on the street in the wee hours of the morning trying to catch a plane home, and as far away from him as possible.

However, she'd give just about anything to see him come barreling around the corner right now.

Brock strode around the corner onto 6th Ave and stopped short. He took in the scene unfolding before him with one quick glance and then ducked back around the corner before he was spotted.

He could be mistaken, it was still pretty dark after all, but he could swear that he'd finally caught up to the woman of his dreams, only to find her about to get on the train with some scrawny, homeless-looking guy hanging on her arm.

Leaning his head back against the wall, he couldn't believe his luck. Had she been playing with him all this time? Messing with his feelings? What about all of those smiles on the plane ride over? And the touching? And the looking?

And the touching?

His chest heaved on a heavy sigh. Somehow he wasn't surprised. What the hell was wrong with people these days? Everyone was so damn selfish. No one cared about other people anymore. About their feelings. Or about how their decisions may affect another person, and the plans they'd made.

Naked plans.

Respectful, but naked, plans.

He thumped the back of his head against the wall and looked toward the heavens for some answers. None were forthcoming.

He sighed again. It didn't matter. He didn't deserve a sweet female like that, anyway. Sooner or later she'd find out the kind of male he really was. Or at least the kind of male everyone thought he was. The circumstances didn't matter. Not in his world. She wouldn't be so keen on him then.

Shoving his hands deep into the front pockets of his jeans, he scowled at the pavement through the curtain of his long hair. Then he shook his head slightly in response to his own self-doubt. No. He wasn't going to give up that easily. He wasn't a bad guy. He wasn't. There were reasons he'd done what he'd done.

Honorable reasons.

And he had plans. Plans that included running his hands and mouth over every single inch of soft skin covering all of those luscious curves of hers. He'd never be able to get her out of his head until he did. The need to fuck her had obsessed him since he'd first laid eyes on her.

An uplifting thought occurred to him: Maybe he was jumping to conclusions. Misreading the situation. He could at least try to have a conversation with her. Find out what was going on. He hadn't come all of this way for nothing.

Besides, he'd saved her life. And her best friend's life. That had to count for something.

His head snapped up, his musings scattering away on the gusty breeze. He could have sworn he'd heard his name. Leaning around the corner, he saw they were just about to get on the light rail.

Heather hesitated in the doorway and looked around, shooting her companion a dirty look when he rudely shoved her and ordered her to get inside.

Had she looked scared? Was she looking for him?

Brock scoffed at himself as soon as the thought crossed his mind, yet somehow, he felt that he wasn't far off the mark. Straightening up off the wall, he rushed toward the train, hopping through the back door right before it closed. Lowering his large frame into the first empty seat he saw, he slouched down and decided to watch and wait. He didn't want to make a fool out of himself. He wanted to know what was going on between them before he'd let his presence there be known.

His eyes narrowed and a possessive growl rumbled in his chest as the homeless guy put his arm around Heather. The only thing that saved the degenerate from a certain immediate death right then and there was the way she stiffened at his touch.

"Is that really necessary?" Heather hissed.

Even though they were sitting more toward the front, Brock had no trouble hearing their conversation. Supernatural canine hearing and all that. Plus, they were the only ones on the train other than a middle-aged couple who still looked half asleep.

The homeless guy chuckled. "Just wanna make sure you don't go anywhere."

Heather grabbed his hand, bent his wrist back, and ducked out from under his arm, shoving it back toward him.

That's my girl.

"Where would I freaking go? I'm not going to jump out of a moving train, even if I could get the doors open."

"It's not like it would permanently hurt you," the homeless guy said.

Huh? Of course it would hurt her.

"Be that as it may," she answered, "I still don't like pain. Not even the temporary kind. I wouldn't purposely inflict it on myself."

The guy leaned in closer to her and lowered his voice until even Brock had to strain to hear him. "Then I strongly suggest you don't give me any trouble. Now that we know you're still alive, there won't be any more hiding from us."

"I realize this, Frank. I'm not stupid." After a pause, she asked, "So, what does this mean? For me? What's going to happen now?"

"You're going to come back to us. The prince will tell you anything else you need to know."

Go back where? Prince of what? What the fuck is this guy talking about?

"What if I don't want to come back?"

"That's not an option."

Heather narrowed her eyes at him. "Oh, there's always another option."

The man stared at her, but she glared right back until he gave her a tight smile and looked away.

They were quiet the rest of the trip, but Brock could tell that Heather was extremely nervous. Scared even. He fought the overwhelming need to follow his heart and swoop in there and rescue her. His head was telling him to bide his time. He would continue to follow them instead, and find out what they were talking about before he saved the girl.

The light rail pulled up to SEA-TAC. Brock slid down lower in his seat until they walked up to the front door and got off, and then he waited until the last second before he jumped out the rear door. He quickly spotted Heather and her friend and set off after them, staying back far enough that he wouldn't be easily noticed.

Surprisingly, they didn't enter the airport, but veered off toward the parking garage instead. The homeless guy, Frank, steered Heather toward a rusted out, green Buick parked about halfway down one of the rows of vehicles. Brock watched as she stood passively while he opened the door for her, but as soon as he let go of her arm, she tried to make a run for it. However he must've been expecting it, for he caught her easily and lifted her into the car like her superior height was nothing to him. Shutting the door, he shook his head at her and waved his hand through the air in front of him. The locks clicked.

Brock heard the locks go down and ducked behind a nearby car. He watched through the windows as she struggled to open her door while Frank casually strolled around the front of the car and got into the driver's side.

As soon as he heard the engine rev, he flagged down

some people that had just parked their truck near him. "I need to borrow your vehicle," he told the man and his young wife.

"What? No! Get the hell out of here. Asshole."

The human had a lot of balls seeing as to how he was a good foot or more shorter than Brock with nowhere near the muscle mass. He had to respect a guy that stood up for himself, even if he was obviously lacking in intelligence, but he didn't have time to play right now.

Letting his wolf out just a bit, his blue eyes became brighter and brighter until they glowed from his face like burning hot flames. He pulled his lips back from his elongated canines, and growled ominously at the human. "Give me your fucking keys."

The man's eyes widened and his mouth dropped open. Sweat popped out on his upper lip. Dropping the keys on the pavement, he turned and ran, leaving his suitcases and his wife behind to fend for herself.

Brock picked the keys up off of the pavement and looked over to see Heather and her companion just pulling out of the garage. "Ma'am," he said politely to the terrified woman standing there next to the luggage. "I'll need you to get out of the way."

She jumped to the side as he hopped in and started the truck, backed it up, and pulled away with a squeal of the tires.

He didn't have to follow them far, just across the highway and into a residential neighborhood. They pulled into the driveway of an ordinary, one-story house with tan siding and flaky white trim. Brock hung back just down the street, pulling over to the side of the small road.

Turning his lights off, he waited to make sure they were going to stay there before he shut off the engine and got out.

This early in the morning, none of the other residents were up and around yet, so there was no need for the vagrant to continue the ruse of being any kind of a nice guy. He kept a firm grip on Heather's upper arm as he yanked her toward the house, forcing her along with him even when she stumbled.

Brock jogged up the street as soon as they disappeared inside, and after a quick scan of the area to make sure no one was watching, he slid around to the side of the house. The back yard was fenced in, so he reached over the gate and felt for the latch. He found it easily and let himself into the backyard.

Leaving it unlatched behind him, he dropped into a crouch and waited, listening for dogs, but none came running to see who was invading their territory. Staying low, he snuck around to the back of the house where he could see in the windows.

Heather was there, standing in the middle of a large kitchen devoid of any furniture. She stood tall with her arms at her sides and her chin lifted as she faced the one in front of her. But he saw her eyes skitter around the room, belying her calm outward demeanor. Behind her were three men, including Frank, the homeless guy who had brought her here.

Brock crept closer until he was right outside the window closest to where she stood and pressed his back against the outside wall, out of sight.

One, two, three!

Twisting around, he took a quick look inside before slamming his back up against the outer wall again.

Other than a block of kitchen knives on the counter, there weren't any weapons in there that he had seen. That would certainly make his rescue a hell of a lot easier. Of course, even if there were, they wouldn't hurt him enough to stop him. But getting stabbed or shot did tend to make him wolf out, and he'd rather not do that in front of her just yet if he could avoid it.

Besides, it ruined his clothes, and he'd just bought these jeans.

His musings were interrupted by the sound of a silvery voice speaking perfect non-accented English.

"An unexpected guest! I'm so glad you could come!"

Brock froze, thinking for a moment that he was speaking to him until he heard Heather mutter, "This was unexpected all right." Squatting down until only his eyes were above the bottom windowpane, he peered through the window again. The guy in front of her was speaking. A tall man with long, white hair and an aquiline nose. He was wearing a black, button down shirt and dress pants, and was quite elegant in his mannerisms. Brock guessed him to be about fifty-ish, more or less. It was hard to tell. Narrowing his eyes in thought, he looked the male up and down again. There was something strangely familiar about him…

The homeless guy with the dirty-blonde hair gave Heather a shove from behind.

"You will kneel before your prince," he spit out.

She gave him a look over her shoulder. "Stop being such a bully, Frank." But doing as he'd ordered, she lowered herself rather gracefully to one knee and tilted her head toward the man's silver-tipped boots.

The "prince" tsk'ed at Frank and smiled down at Heather. "There is no need for that, daughter. Forgive him. You may rise."

Daughter?

She rose to her feet but kept her head down.

Lines of worry were etched on Brock's forehead. Even in the short time he'd known her, he knew that being so well behaved wasn't like her at all. He could see her chest rising and falling with each rapid breath and knew she was frightened. But other than the rude one who'd brought her here, he couldn't see what was so scary about these guys. They looked perfectly pleasant to him.

It was really a shame that he was going to have to pound them all through that pretty hardwood floor.

CHAPTER 4

Heather looked up through her lashes at the prince of her people. He wasn't what she had expected at all from her parent's stories. As a matter of fact, he appeared almost...kind. But if she paid attention, she could sense the undercurrent of supremacy he carried within him simmering just beneath the surface, and she saw no mercy in his dark eyes.

Her chest felt tight as she tried to breathe, and she wondered for the upteenth time what the hell had possessed her to leave the safety of the apartments she'd been staying in to go wandering off on her own like an idiot.

"Where are your mother and father?" the prince asked her.

Yeah, like there was any chance in hell she was going to tell him that. She licked her dry lips as she thought about how best to answer his question without angering him.

Deciding that honesty would probably be the best policy in this situation, she lifted her chin and looked him square in the eyes. "I respectfully decline to answer that question, sir. Prince. Sir Prince." She cleared her throat. "I love my parents dearly, and there is nothing you can do or say that will make me give them up to you."

One side of his mouth couldn't seem to decide if he wanted to smile or not. Either he was mildly amused, or he was so appalled at her lack of regard for his royal godness that he had acquired an uncontrollable tick.

"Strangely enough, I don't believe you would," he murmured after a long moment, saying more loudly, "And I do appreciate your honesty." He linked his hands together and did smile then. His teeth were straight and white and perfect. Too perfect. "I'm only inquiring as to how they are. I mean them no harm." He looked at her expectantly.

All the little hairs stood up on the back of her neck. She took a fortifying gulp of air and steeled herself. "Still ain't happening," she told him firmly. Closing her eyes tight, she braced herself for the repercussions that were sure to follow such a blatant show of defiance.

When long seconds passed and all of her limbs were still attached, she cracked open one eye and peaked out at him.

He arched an eyebrow in question. Coldly amused this time.

"Aren't you going to smite me or something?" she asked.

That bone-chilling smile widened until it almost

reached his eyes. "Smite you?" He chuckled. "No, Heather. I'm not going to smite you. I need you."

It was her turn to arch a delicate brow. "Need me? Need me for what?"

"I need you to help our people."

She frowned. "I'm not sure I'm the best person to come to about something like that. I've been gone for a long time. What could I possibly do to help any of you?"

The prince continued to smile as he clasped his hands behind his back and began to pace, glancing at her every now and then out of the corner of his eye. "Well, I did have some grand plans involving a lovely wedding to a very handsome, if albeit a bit violent, lad to help unite our tribes, however, another option has just made itself known to me. A much more desirable option than making nice with those miscreants."

The smile abruptly fell from his face and he turned his head toward the window.

"You may come in now, wolf," he called out in a singsong voice.

Heather's head snapped around. She couldn't see anything at first with the light from the kitchen reflecting on the glass. Not until he stood up to his full height and Brock's impressive form filled the entire frame.

His blue eyes found hers, and his were narrowed with concern. Or was that suspicion? He let himself in through the open back door and strode confidently into the room to stand next to her with his shoulders back and his hands at his sides.

Her memory hadn't done justice as to just how good-looking and charismatic he was. With his long hair and close-cut beard, he looked like a sexy lumberjack, or a biker (more like Sons of Anarchy than Hell's Angels). She'd also forgotten how large he was. Or maybe he just seemed taller standing in this room with all of these average height males. He even stood a good five inches taller than the prince, and was at least twice his girth. As she watched, the muscles in his arms and chest twitched under his tee shirt, like he was having a hard time standing still.

"Welcome to our little get together," the prince said. "What is your name, canine?"

Brock's narrowed eyes shifted from her to the prince at the demeaning classification. He seemed to ignore the other three men in the room. "Brock."

"Brock…of course. A fine name for a strong male." The prince strolled in a circle around him, his eyes roaming over every inch of Brock's muscular body. Eventually, he came to a stop directly in front of him, but stayed just out of arms reach. "Why are you here? What is this female to you?"

Heather felt her face flame as Brock blinked in surprise. She'd only known him for a few days. She wasn't anything to him.

"I'm sorry?" Brock asked, glancing her way.

The prince waited until he had Brock's full attention. Catching his eyes and holding them with his own, he said in a low voice, "I think you heard me. Now kindly answer the question."

As if he couldn't help himself, Brock's eyes wandered back to her and travelled hungrily from the top of her head to the tips of her sneakers and back. "I want to fuck her," he announced to the room. "More than any other woman I've ever met."

Heather swallowed loudly, taken aback by his bluntness even as an answering ache blossomed low in her belly. Her blood began to pound as her body responded to the hunger in his eyes. Her breasts swelled under his gaze, the nipples straining toward him, and a surge of moisture wet her panties.

His eyes on her breasts, he growled deep in his throat. She had to bite the inside of her cheek to keep from moaning in response. Then he blinked, and shook his head slightly, looking chagrined as he apologized to her. "I'm sorry, I don't know why I said that." His eyes swept over her of their own accord one last time, and his nostrils flared before he tore his gaze away and turned his attention back to the prince.

The prince nodded, his expression thoughtful as he muttered, "You said it because it is the honest truth, and the only kind of answer I allowed you to give. Now, the question is, how badly do you want her?"

"Why do you need to know?" Brock asked. "What is this about?"

The prince moved closer and the wolf lifted his face as he neared, scenting the air. His heavy brows came together. "Who are you?" he asked. "*What* are you?"

The room fell silent as the prince searched Brock's features, and then turned to pace the floor without answering him, one hand rubbing his chin thoughtfully.

Frank spoke up from his post behind Heather. "Your majesty, I don't think this is a good idea. We don't need him, or any of his kind. Let's dispose of him now and be on our way."

One of the others, a handsome, balding man in a suit, spoke up. "I disagree. We could use all of the help we can get. If this male can get other shifters on our side, we may actually have a chance."

The prince nodded as they spoke, appearing to consider what they were saying. He continued to pace for another few minutes while they all waited in silence. Then he came to an abrupt halt and faced the group. His eyes were lit from within and gleaming like a madman as he studied them, colors swirling off and on in the dark irises like those hypnotic spirals that never ended.

This couldn't be good.

With a maniacal smile he said, "We will let fate decide." Reaching into his pocket, he pulled out a gold coin. "Call it, wolf."

Brock looked around the room. "What the fook is going on?!" he bellowed with rising anxiety, a slight Scottish brogue suddenly appearing in his dialect.

Heather cringed. It appeared his patience was at an end. She wanted to reassure him, but it was kind of hard when she had no idea what was happening herself.

"It's quite simple," the prince told him. "Heads, you win. Tails, you die. Now, CALL IT." He threw the coin in the air.

"Heads!" Brock called, looking as if all of the world had gone mad. Which it kind of had.

Heather held her breath as the prince caught the coin and flipped it over onto the back of his opposite hand.

He seemed a tiny bit surprised as he said, "Today is your lucky day, wolf. You won."

A deep rumble filled the room before he'd even finished speaking. Brock's chest was heaving, his muscles were twitching, and his chin was lowered as he caught the prince in his hunter's stare. "You will tell me who you are, and whit th' fook is going on. Right now. 'Afore I lose my shit."

Ignoring him completely, the prince smiled fondly at Heather. "Are you ready, my dear?"

She turned frantic eyes to him, "Ready for what?"

The prince raised his hands in front of him, palms facing each other. "And…go!" He clapped his hands together twice in quick succession.

The room began to spin around her and the floor shifted under her feet. Throwing her arms out to the sides, she frantically reached out toward the only one in the room that seemed somewhat sane. "Brock!"

"Heather!" he roared.

His long hair whipped around his face as he dove toward her. But just as he was about to grab her hand, she felt herself get grabbed from behind and she was yanked off the floor and sucked backwards.

She screamed as she was surrounded by darkness.

CHAPTER 5

Brock threw himself toward Heather as the room and everything in it spun around them with rapidly increasing speed, but just as he made a grab for her, she screamed as she was sucked back into a black void that had opened up behind her.

"Noooooo!" he yelled as her fingertips brushed his. She was gone before he could get a grip on her. He threw his hands out in front of him to catch himself as he hit the floor, but his body paused, hovering in midair as the world around him changed direction. Something grabbed him from behind, the force of it bending his body at the waist as he was sucked back the opposite way.

His hair blew around his head, obstructing his view. Not that there was much to see. Tumbling head over heels, he careened through the abyss, trying to catch his breath as the cold air whipped around him. It was like he'd gotten sucked into the middle of a black hole.

After what seemed like hours but was more likely only

seconds, he felt gravity take hold, pulling him in the opposite direction as he sped through the blackness. He panicked and his wolf howled, responding to the adrenalin flooding through him. Throwing his arms and legs straight out, he settled into a free-fall and allowed the change to take him without fighting it. If anything had a chance of surviving this, it was his wolf.

He roared as his bones shifted inside of him in mid-air, reforming and resetting. His skin stretched and his muscles tore and healed as they grew into his new shape. Sun-tipped fur sprang out in sparse tufts until it covered his entire body.

The change complete, he opened his eyes just in time to see the ground rushing up at him. He hit hard, unprepared, the earth cracking beneath him with the force of his landing. Tumbling over and over until he slowed enough to come up on all fours, he dropped back down into a defensive crouch and bared his dagger-like teeth in a snarl, prepared for anything. His eyes skittered this way and that, but he couldn't see much through the thick fog that rolled over the ground.

Still keeping a wary eye, he lowered his head and sniffed. He smelled pine and dirt and decaying insects. Around him, all he saw were the ghostly silhouettes of evergreens. It was eerily quiet. He heard no birds, no animals, no rustling of the trees. Nothing.

What the hell was he supposed to do here? And where was Heather?

As if in answer to his unspoken question, a scrap of paper floated to the ground in front of him.

Brock snarled and reared up onto his hind legs. He

spun around in a tight circle, looking for the one who'd dropped the note, but he could perceive no immediate threat. With one last cautious sniff at the air, he began to change back to his human form. He didn't make a sound, more in control of the process this time in spite of the pain. When it was finished, he caught his breath and bent down and picked up the paper. Pushing his hair back off his face, he read the elegant script on the page.

"Find the girl and return to where you started. You have five days."

He looked around again, and then glanced down at himself. His clothes had been ripped to shreds on his way down. He could see a few pieces of material hanging from the tree branches, while the rest lay strewn across the ground like the remnants of a plane crash. What was he supposed to do? Just run around naked? Personally, he could really care less about his nudity, but it may disturb anyone else he happened to run into.

He heard a small thud behind him and he turned to find a golden coin lying on the ground, identical to the one the prince had thrown.

"You have got to be fucking kidding me."

He stared at it for long seconds, took a step toward it, and then changed his mind. Leaning his head back, he yelled to the sky, "Can't I just have some clothes?"

The coin gleamed with an odd light from its spot in the grass, even with no sun. Brock stared at it some more, paced back and forth a few times without taking his eyes from it, and then stopped in front of it again.

Well, might as well see what the fuck this was all about. Somehow, he had a feeling that he wouldn't be able to get away with *not* tossing the stupid coin. Picking it up, he tossed it high. As it began to fall back toward him, he shouted, "Tails!" Catching the coin, he flipped it over onto the back of his opposite hand.

An etching of a pine tree stared back at him. It was tails.

Something landed behind him and he spun around to find a pair of camouflage cargo pants, a black tee shirt, thick-soled combat boots, and some heavy socks all wrapped in a sheet of plastic.

Tearing it open, he got dressed. He waited a few minutes to see if anything else was going to fall, but apparently, this was all he was going to get. He tucked the note and the coin into his pocket.

This was like a bad game of the Alice in Wonderland sort. He didn't have a fucking clue where to start searching for Heather, or how to find his way back here once he found her. And this fog was so thick, he couldn't see more than ten or fifteen feet in front of him.

But he did know that he would be no good to anyone if he didn't cover the basics. So first, he needed to find water, and food.

Picking up a few pieces of his destroyed shirt, he tore off a small strip and tied a marker to one of the tree branches to his right. Then he repeated the process on a tree on his left to mark the spot where he'd landed. The crack in the ground would be his third clue. He shoved the rest in his pocket and set off in no particular direction.

He'd been walking for a few hours when he heard what he'd been hoping for: The sound of trickling water.

Veering off to the right, he topped a small rise and saw a small stream dead ahead. It wasn't much, but it would do.

Like any animal, he knew that if there were one place he would run into trouble, it would be approaching a water source without checking for others who were doing the same thing. So he tied a strip of material to a branch to mark the spot where he'd veered from his trail, but stuck to the trees for a few minutes, watching and listening. When he was sure the coast was clear, he cautiously left his cover.

He looked around carefully one more time before dropping to his knees and cupping his hands in the icy water. Taking a small sip, he let it run over his tongue and then spit it out, waiting for any possible ill effects. After a minute or two, he still felt fine, so he drank in earnest this time, then splashed some cold water on his face.

Deciding to stay near the water source as he had nothing to carry it in, he followed it downstream until it started to get dark. He found a clump of trees that would provide some shelter, stripped off his clothes, and left them folded neatly against one of the trunks.

He needed to hunt and find some food.

Even in wolf form, it took him another few hours to find a small animal. He wasn't even sure what it was, but it appeared to be edible. Taking it back to his shelter, he hunkered down for the night with his meal. The temperature had dropped, and he debated turning back and putting his clothes back on, but decided against it. He'd be better able to defend himself in his current form if any type of danger stumbled upon him during the night.

Not for the first time that day, a familiar feeling of

loneliness swept over him. He had no idea how he was supposed to find Heather. He'd been tromping through this God-forsaken place all day. All he'd seen were pine trees, fog, and the stream. This animal he'd caught was the first warm-blooded creature he'd come across, and he'd had to dig it out of a burrow.

Hell, he didn't even know if he was going the right way. Or if Heather was even really here, wherever the fuck "here" was. Or if she was the "girl" he was supposed to find. He assumed so, but who knew with all the shit that was going on?

He wondered, again, who this guy was that had sent him here. One thing was for sure: The dude had to be some kind of powerful witch to pull off something like this, and Brock hated witches. They gave him the creeps, and he tried like hell to avoid them. It was no wonder he'd made his skin crawl.

But that prince…that prince had seemed vaguely familiar to him, like he'd met him somewhere before, but he didn't see how that could've happened. He shook his head, ruffling his fur. Nah, there was no way he could know him. Yet, for some reason, he was positive that he did.

Tired and frustrated, he laid his head on his pile of clothing and tried to get some sleep.

* * *

AFTER A LONG, lonely night, morning crept up on him along with that fucking, never-ending fog. Brock stood up and shook the pine needles out of his fur, then trotted over to the stream for a drink. He finished the meat he'd saved for breakfast, changed back to human form, and pulled his clothes on. Kicking at the ground, he covered up any trace of his having crashed there. He even buried the remains of his dinner/breakfast.

This place appeared to be all peaceful and surreal, but he didn't trust it for a minute. His instincts were telling him it was a shit storm waiting to happen. The only thing he didn't know was when or where.

Without any better options presenting themselves, he continued to follow the stream.

A FEW HOURS LATER, he found her.

CHAPTER 6

Tears wet Heather's cheeks as she huddled in the small cave she'd found, if you could call it that. It was more like a really large burrow, dug into a small hillside at the base of a giant tree. She swiped them away angrily. She was cold, she was sore, she was hungry, she was thirsty, and she needed a freaking toothbrush.

She pulled out her phone for the hundredth time. Duck walking to the entrance of the cave, she held it up in the air, trying to find a signal. Nothing. And to make matters worse, if that was even possible, the battery was about to die.

Frustrated beyond reason, she threw it up against the rocks at the back of her hideout, then immediately burst into tears at the depth of stupidity she'd just fallen to by smashing her only possible connection to the outside world.

She sat there until she was all cried out, then with a loud sniff, she wiped off her face. It was getting lighter out, which meant morning was finally here, and unless she planned on dying in this cave, she needed to get herself together and take some action.

Thing was, she wasn't used to taking action. Not for her own survival anyway. At the risk of sounding like a spoiled brat, which she supposed she kind of was, she had to admit that her parents had always taken care of everything for her, ever since she was a kid. They'd even found the apartment she currently lived in, and helped her get the job she wanted so she could work with Gracie. She'd never wanted for anything, and she was very grateful to them for that.

However, as a result, her survival skills were practically non-existent. And she'd been living as a human for so long, her other skills were unused and long forgotten. Even her accelerated healing had taken her by surprise after she'd landed here in a heap of broken bones and lacerations. She'd passed out, sure she was going to die a horrible and painful death all alone in the middle of this haunted forest. But when she'd regained consciousness, many of her cuts and abrasions had already healed, and though she'd still had some broken bones, she'd been able to drag herself over to this little cave.

Her stomach growled loudly. Right. Food. Water would be good too. She peered into the gloomy morning. If this fog got any heavier, she'd be able to just stick her tongue out to quench her thirst, but until then, she'd need to find another source.

Stepping out of the cave for the first time since she'd found it two days ago, she brushed the dirt off of her yoga pants and tee shirt and zipped up her running jacket. She ran her shaky fingers through her long, brown hair and tried to get out the worst of the tangles. Another tear snuck down her cheek as she thought about her shower at home.

Stop it, she chided herself. *Crying has done nothing at all for you so far except make your eyes hurt and give you a headache.*

She stared out at the never-ending fog and her mind wandered, as it often had over the past hours, to Brock. Was he here too? Somewhere? Wandering around lost and alone?

She wondered if he was looking for her. Would he even know to look for her? Well, in any case, she couldn't just sit around here and wait for a man to save her. She needed to save herself.

She looked around with a forlorn expression. Dammit. That had sounded so good in her head.

Come on, Heather, you're a strong, independent woman. Stop whining and go find yourself some food and water.

In spite of her strong self-conviction, questions continued to swirl around in her head until it began to ache anew. All of this had been caused by something as insignificant as a coin toss. Of course, the other option had been immediate death for her werewolf. And possibly for her. But what was the point?

The Fae were freaking strange creatures. And the prince was the strangest of them all. Her parents had warned her. They believed his age was making him a bit mad, and when his decisions for their people had become more and more dubious to them, they'd taken Heather and run away. They'd said they'd rather live their lives amongst the humans than with an unpredictable monarch leading them. But she'd had no idea what to expect if she ever ran across him. Not truly.

She supposed after living such a long life, it was hard to find things to amuse yourself, but she sincerely hoped she wouldn't stoop to messing with people's lives like this when she got to his age, if she managed to live that long.

Her thoughts circled back around to Brock, as they were wont to do. If she ever saw him again, she owed him a huge apology.

The mist suddenly stirred in front of her and as if she'd conjured him up with her wishful thinking, he stepped through the fog not five feet away from her. She noticed he was wearing different clothes. Maybe she was still unconscious and only dreaming of him after all.

Heather stared, then squeezed her eyes shut, counted to five, and opened them again. She even pinched her arm, just to be sure.

He was still there.

Fresh tears pooled in her eyes as he gave her a relieved smile and held out his big arms to her.

She wasted no more time standing there by herself. Running over to him, she let him enfold her in his warm embrace, wrapping her arms around his lean waist and hanging on tight. She shoved her face into his chest as fresh sobs racked her body. "I'm so-so-sor-sorry."

"Shhhh," he said. One large hand smoothed her tangled hair down her back as the other held her tight. "It's all right, sunshine. I'm here."

Heather cried herself out for the second time since she'd woken up. To his credit, he didn't try to stop her, but just let her get it all out. When she could breathe normally again, she leaned back just far enough to scowl up at him. "What the hell took you so long?"

He barked out a laugh and pulled her close again. "Sorry. Next time we're sucked out of our time and thrown into a new dimension or whatever the hell this is, I'll endeavor to find you sooner."

She sniffed and wiped her face on his shirt. "You don't happen to have any water, do you? Or food?"

It was his turn to scowl down at her. "Food is scarce, but there's water. You haven't had any?"

She shook her head against his hard chest. "I was just about to go look."

One arm still draped around her shoulders, he stepped back and pointed in the direction he'd come from. "There's a fresh stream about a hundred yards that way. Can't you hear it?"

She sniffed, listened, and then shook her head again. Had she really been licking the moisture off of the rocks all this time when water was so close?

Oh my God, I really am a loser. Of course, it would've taken her an entire day to crawl over to it and back in the condition she'd been in.

Grabbing her by the hand, he started off in that direction, pulling her along behind him. As they walked, he asked, "Have you been here the whole time? In this cave?"

She bristled at his tone. "I told you. I was just about to go start exploring when you showed up."

"But you've been here for nearly two days? Without trying to find water? Or food? Not in all that time?"

She changed the subject. "How did you find me?"

"I smelled you."

They arrived at the stream and Heather fell gratefully to her knees to drink. The water was like ice, and her hands were blue by the time she'd gotten her fill. While she was down there, she gave her underarm a discreet sniff. She didn't smell that bad yet, did she? "It's not my fault there are no showers here."

He laughed again. "No, sunshine. You smell like heather."

"Um…yeah?"

"Like the foliage, not your name."

"Like the flowers? In Scotland?"

"Yes. The blossoms don't have a strong smell, but it's there."

Is that why her parents had given her that name? They couldn't come up with something more original?

"By the way, I love the smell of heather," he said with a wink. "Reminds me of home."

She wasn't sure what to say to that, so she stood up again and bent over to brush off her knees. "What do we do now?"

He remained silent for so long that she finally looked up at him in question. The heat in his blue eyes as he stared at her chest took her by surprise, and warmth flooded through her to pool in her lower belly. Her large breasts never failed to get attention from the men she ran across, whether they were attracted to the rest of her or not, but the fact that they got *his* attention made a warm feeling unfold in her belly. She cleared her throat, breaking the spell.

He blinked and looked up, grinning at her and shrugging without shame when he realized that she'd caught him staring.

Taking her by the hand again, he studied the area around them. "I haven't eaten yet today either, so how about I go rustle us up some grub? We can eat before we head back."

"Head back to where?" she asked as they started back to the cave. Her voice sounded husky, even to her own ears. She cleared her throat again.

"According to my instructions, I'm supposed to find you and go back to where I crash landed." He stopped suddenly and spun around to face her. He took her by the shoulders. "Jesus. I didn't even ask. Are you okay? If you arrived here anywhere near as hard as I did..." His face screwed up at the thought and he immediately started checking her for injuries.

She tried to reassure him as he ran his hands down her arms and up her legs, feeling for breaks that had already healed, swatting at him when he got too close to the junction between her thighs. "I'm fine. Really." *Now.* "I just kind of floated here..." *Like an anvil in the cartoons.*

He didn't need to know that the reason she'd been hiding in the cave for two days was because she'd dragged herself there after breaking numerous bones upon her arrival, and it had taken that long for her to heal.

He straightened up with obvious reluctance, his eyes continuing to rove over her with concern.

She cocked an eyebrow at him. "Really. I'm fine. You have instructions?"

Brock pulled a slip of paper out of his pocket and handed it to her.

She read it out loud. "Find the girl and return to where you started. You have five days." She handed it back to him with a snort. "Dramatic much?"

Brock started walking again, taking her hand and pulling her along with him. "Well, anyone who can send us through space and time to a different place with nothing but a clap of their hands is someone who can be as dramatic as they please as far as I'm concerned."

"I'm perfectly capable of walking on my own, you know," she told him.

He gave her a puzzled look and she held up their linked hands. But instead of letting her go, he scowled and tightened his hold. "I don't want you to 'shoosh' away from me again."

They reached the cave and he ushered her inside before telling her with obvious reluctance, "Wait in here for me. I won't be long." He started to leave, but paused to tell her, "Hang on to the wall if things start getting weird. Or a rock. A heavy one. Don't go anywhere."

Heather ducked through the opening and stepped inside, turning around to face him again. "Why can't I just come with you?"

"Oh. Uh…" He dropped his head, hiding behind his long hair as he rubbed an imaginary dirty spot off of one muscular forearm. "Because I hunt in my…uh…other form."

"Oh." She really didn't want to be alone again. "Do you have to hunt like that? Can't you do it…like this?" She waved her hand around, indicating his current human, and very attractive, form.

He glanced up at her with sheepish blue eyes. "Um,

well, it would be kind of hard to catch something with my bare hands. Teeth are easier."

She could see his point. "Other than hanging on to something and/or anchoring myself down, what am I supposed to do while you're gone?"

His rugged face lit up with a naughty smile, and she saw a flash of white teeth. "Watch my clothes."

"Watch your…oh." She stared in awe as he shrugged out of his shirt, revealing row upon row of rippling abdominal muscles, a hard chest, and defined biceps under smooth, golden skin. There wasn't an ounce of fat on him.

How was that even fair?

He folded up his tee shirt and stuck it under one powerful arm, then bent over to unlace his boots. Kicking them off one at a time, he stuffed his socks inside of them. Handing her his shirt, he suggested with a wink, "You may want to turn around for this next part. At least until we get to know each other better."

Her eyes widened as his hands went to the waistband of his pants. His long fingers popped open the button and yanked the zipper down. Sliding his hands under the material and over his narrow hips, he pushed them down his strong thighs and muscular calves, his long hair covering his manliest parts as he bent over to pull them off each leg.

Heather spun around before he stood up again and caught her gawking like a virgin. But, *damn*. He looked even better naked, if that were possible.

Warm breath stirred the hair on the back of her head. She stiffened, knowing he was so close…and wearing absolutely nothing. Her heart sped up as he reached over her shoulder to hand her his folded pants.

His deep voice rumbled near her ear, causing goose flesh to rise up all over her body. "Stay here. I'll be back as soon as I can."

She caught her breath as he straightened up, but then lowered his nose to her hair, inhaling deeply, and then the warmth behind her was gone. She waited a few seconds before turning around.

A large wolf/human hybrid stood just inside the fog, more muscular than a normal wolf and more animal than human. It was twice Brock's human size and covered with sparse, sun-kissed brown fur. Its back muscles twitched, its sapphire blue eyes staring at her intently as she stood there hugging his clothes to her chest. Then it ambled away on four legs to go find their breakfast.

Had he been gauging her reaction? Maybe she should've acted more shocked. Or afraid? But honestly, he was a magnificent beast; in either form.

Lifting his clothes to her nose, she inhaled his scent. He smelled faintly of fresh pine and clean air and something masculine and woodsy that she couldn't quite put her finger on. It made her want to rub his clothes all over her bare skin. Or better yet, rub *him* all over her bare skin.

She never should have made that promise to Grace when he'd first shown up at her apartment after following her friend there. The one where she'd told her she would stay away from him.

Although she didn't think it should really apply anymore anyway. Actually, now that she thought about it, she'd only told her best friend that she would stay away from him "for now".

It wasn't now anymore. It was later. Much later. *Days* later. And besides, it didn't count if you were in a different world.

CHAPTER 7

Brock trotted back to the cave with his kill in his mouth. He'd found a nice, fat, whatever-this-thing-was less than two miles away. It was plenty large enough to feed the both of them until dinner.

Maybe they should just hang out here for the day. They had plenty of time to get back to "where he started". It had taken him less than two days in human form, and he'd marked his trail well. That gave them three days to get back. It should be easy, even if the going was a bit slower with Heather along.

Besides, that woman had some explaining to do. From what he'd overheard outside of that house, she wasn't a normal, human female. And those men weren't just men. He'd gotten the same vibe from them that he'd gotten from the prince.

That feeling of familiarity came over him again. He racked his brain, thinking of every supernatural creature he'd ever seen, hoping something would come to him, but he couldn't think of anything that was capable of what the "prince" had done to him and Heather. As a matter of fact, he was positive that he'd never so much as heard of anything that could do that, except a witch. So there was no way he could've met this man before.

He wondered for the hundredth time what, exactly, the point was of sending them to this place. This challenge, or game, or whatever it was, couldn't be this easy. Something bad was going to happen. He could feel it.

His senses were on high alert as Heather's little cave came into sight through the fog. She was sitting in the entrance with her legs crossed in front of her and her chin in her hands. Wisps of her soft hair trailed in waves across her face. She swiped at it crossly. Her despondent sigh carried across the distance to him as she traced a pattern on her knee with her finger. He noticed she had pulled a rather large rock next to her and a snuffling sound, half amusement and half approval, came from his muzzle.

He sniffed the air and looked around. He didn't see or smell anything threatening, so he trotted up to the cave, not too fast so as not to spook her, and dropped his kill in the dirt by her foot.

His caution appeared to be unnecessary. She didn't appear frightened of him at all, but her welcoming smile quickly turned into a grimace as she glanced down at his offering. "What is that? Is that a cat?" she asked in horror. She shook her head hard. "Oh, hell no. I can't eat a cat."

Tilting his head, he looked at it, trying to see it through her eyes. He supposed it did look a bit like a short-tailed cat. Kind of like a skunk/woodchuck/cat...thing. A skoochat.

He picked up his clothes in his teeth and went far enough around the tree outside of the cave that she couldn't see, or hear, him. Closing his eyes, he willed himself to change back, gritting his teeth against the pain so she wouldn't hear.

Changing was never fun, but it was dangerous to stay in his wolf form for too long. The animal instincts would start to take over, his mind would stop thinking like a human and more and more like a lone predator at the top of the food chain, and he would become a danger to anything and anyone around him.

Including Heather.

He pulled on his shirt and pants and padded barefoot back to where she still sat staring at the skoochat. Trying not to laugh, he watched as she tentatively poked at it with a stick. Her cute little nose wrinkled up in repugnance and she threw the stick down.

"It doesn't taste bad," he said, trying to reassure her. "Kind of like chicken." He didn't add the "raw" part.

She jumped slightly at the sound of his voice, and her eyes ran over him. Looking for lingering remnants of fur he was sure, then she went back to eyeballing their breakfast. "For a big guy, you're awfully quiet when you walk."

Sitting down next to her, he pulled on his socks and his boots. "I was thinking we could hang out here for a while today. Get you fed. Strengthen you up a bit before we head back. You look exhausted."

"I told you, I'm not eating that."

He had to admit, it didn't look nearly as appetizing while in his human form. He was going to have to cook it this time.

He patted her thigh in sympathy, then he got up and started gathering some tinder and sticks that were lying inside the cave. Hopefully they were dry enough to get a fire going.

Heather stood up also. "What are you doing?"

"Collecting firewood so we can cook the skoochat."

She crossed her arms over her ample chest. "I'm *not* eating that."

"You need to eat, sunshine."

"I'll be fine."

"I know. Because you're going to eat. Be right back." He left her there to pout and jogged down to the stream. If he remembered correctly, he thought he'd seen some quartz rock just upstream a bit.

When he returned, Heather was sitting back down against the wall near his pile of sticks. She watched silently as he struck the rocks together until he created sparks, lighting the tinder.

He blew on it gently until a tiny fire appeared. Little by little, he fed the flame until he had a small, but strong, fire. Grabbing their breakfast, he stuck it on the end of a makeshift spit and held it over the flame.

Heather refused to watch, lowering her head onto her knees and covering her face with her arms.

But once the fur had burned off and the meat began to cook, an appetizing smell filled the little cave, making his mouth water in anticipation.

Heather's stomach growled loud enough to be heard back home and he had to bite back a smile.

Out of the corner of his eye, he saw her move closer to the fire little by little until she was sitting right next to him. He turned the meat a few more times just to tease her before pulling it out of the fire and blowing on it.

Taking a big bite, he closed his eyes as he chewed. "Mmm," he groaned, wiping off the grease with the back of his arm before it dripped into his beard. He took another bite, smacking his lips and watching her out of the corner of his eye.

She swallowed and licked her lips. "Aren't you gonna offer me some of that?" she asked.

"I thought you weren't eating it."

"Maybe I changed my mind."

He thought about holding out a little longer, just to teach her a lesson, but he found that he just couldn't deny those big, hungry eyes.

He handed her the stick. "Here. You can have the rest."

"Thank you." She grabbed it from his hand and sank her teeth into the tender meat, ripping off a big chunk. Taking another bite before she'd even swallowed the first, she glanced up to find him watching her, his blue eyes sparkling with amusement.

A flush stole up her neck and onto her cheeks, and she dropped her eyes, taking a smaller bite and chewing slower this time.

He laughed. "Don't be embarrassed. It's good to see a woman eat like she means it."

"Yeah? Well, you'll love hanging around me, because as you can plainly see, I don't skip any meals." She patted her belly and grinned.

He didn't care for the implication she was making with that joke. Did she not know how attractive she was? She'd always come across to him as being so confident and sure of herself. Speaking out loud without really meaning to, Brock told her honestly, "Don't put yourself down like that. I think you're one of the sexiest women I've ever seen."

She stopped eating mid-chew and slowly raised her eyes to his. After a moment, she covered her mouth with her hand. "What?" she asked from behind her palm.

Well, it was out there now. No sense in pretending he hadn't said it. Besides, he'd meant every single word. "You heard me."

Swallowing hard, she said, "Yes, but I think I may have misunderstood you."

He gave her a roguish grin. "You didn't misunderstand, Heather. It broke my heart when you ran away. That's why I followed you."

She cocked an eyebrow. He could see she didn't believe him in the slightest. "I think you just like to follow people. So you can practice your tracking skills or something. First, following Grace to my apartment, then me…"

He didn't want to talk about Grace. "Why did you run away?" he asked. "Why come all the way from China to Seattle to see that your best friend made it here safely, just to leave again a few hours after we arrive?"

"I think you know the answer to that."

"Because of what I am." It wasn't a question.

She looked away. Tossing the bones and the stick into the fire, she wiped her hands off on her pants. Her silence was telling.

That's what he'd been afraid of. But what he didn't understand was, why? She'd just proven that she wasn't disgusted by his shifter abilities, or frightened of him.

"Okay." He turned to face her, crossing his long legs in front of him. Picking up her hand, he tucked it between both of his.

She hid behind her hair a bit, but didn't try to pull away.

He ducked his head and watched her face as he said, just to be sure, "Well, it's not because you're frightened of me."

She shook her head no.

He scooted a little closer, until his leg was touching her hip.

This time her back straightened, and she tried to take her hand back. But he wouldn't let her.

"If you're not frightened of me," He leaned in to smell her thick hair, his voice dropping to a husky rumble. "Then why are you fighting what's between us? Why did you run? Unless you wanted me to chase you."

"I had to," she admitted breathlessly.

Brushing her hair back away from the soft skin of her face and behind her shoulder, he nuzzled the side of her neck. "Why? Who are you, sunshine?" Mmmm. She smelled delicious. He dropped a light kiss on her neck, then ran his nose along the shell of her ear, nipping her earlobe. "Tell me."

Her hand tightened around his, and he lifted his other one to cup her cheek, gently turning her face toward his. He kissed her cheek, her jaw, the corner of her sweet mouth. "Because I can't get you out of my head ever since you opened your door to me."

"Brock," she breathed.

He didn't let her finish. He couldn't wait any longer,

and he'd completely forgotten whatever the hell he'd been trying to ask her anyway. Gently, he pulled her head the rest of the way around and claimed her mouth with his. At the first touch of her soft lips, a low moan escaped him, echoed by one of her own as he began to move his mouth with more insistence over hers.

He bit her lower lip and she gasped, giving him access to the warm, velvety inside of her mouth. Thrusting his tongue inside, he tasted her, and his wolf growled within him. It wanted more of this female.

And he agreed wholeheartedly.

She twisted her body toward him, her free hand moving up over his shirt and across his hard chest to grip the top of his shoulder. He continued to ravage her mouth, kissing her until she was leaning into him of her own accord, her moans mixing with his, feeding his lust.

With a growl, he reached around and gripped her by the hips, lifting her with ease and pulling her over on top of him. She seated herself on his lap, one knee on either side of his hips, and his eyes nearly rolled back in his head as she sank down against his erection. The yoga pants she was wearing may as well have been nothing. They were no barrier at all. He could feel her heat, even through his cargo pants.

Placing her hands on his shoulders, she lifted herself up off of him. He growled with frustration, thinking she was leaving him, and gripped her full hips tighter. But then she slid down him again, rubbing herself against his hardness.

Reaching up, he slid his hands through her hair to hold her head still and pulled her mouth back to his as she rolled her hips against him. Her breath was coming in short gasps, and he started to shake, his wolf pacing, his muscles tensing. He fought to restrain himself, but he was losing the battle with every slide of her hips.

Holy fuck. He was about to come, and they still had their clothes on.

Desperately, he tore his mouth from hers and hugged her to him, trying to keep her still long enough for him to distract himself. Her heart pounded hard against his chest, and she moaned in disappointment.

"Sunshine," he gasped and then groaned as she wiggled against him. "Who was that man that sent us here?"

She stilled, her breasts heaving. "What?"

Pulling back to look at her, he pushed her hair out of her eyes. "That man. Who is he?"

Her expression gave nothing away as she stared at him. "Is that what this is all about?"

He frowned in confusion. "What do you mean?"

With a sad smile, she pushed herself up off his lap and stood up.

"Where are you going?" he asked, reaching for her.

She gave him a sarcastic smile. "I can't believe I was so stupid."

He remained on the ground, hoping she'd come back. When she didn't, he asked, "What are you talking about?"

She straightened her clothes and turned back around to face him. Her eyes were cold and hard as she said, "You don't have to play these games to seduce the information out of me. You could just ask."

Games? He couldn't believe she would think that. "I'm not playing games, Heather."

She narrowed her eyes at him and wrapped her arms around herself.

So, this was going to take some convincing. His wolf nearly howled out loud in anticipation. There was nothing it liked more than the hunt. Rising to his feet, he stalked her as she retreated, trying to keep some distance between them. He had to keep his head down so he wouldn't hit the top of the little cave.

Her back hit the wall behind her, and her eyes widened with every step he took as she watched him come closer and closer. She put out her hands to hold him off, but he ignored her meager attempt to keep him away.

Placing one hand on either side of her shoulders, he caged her in and lowered his head until his mouth was next to her ear. "Sunshine," he whispered. "You've got it all wrong." He nipped at her jaw. "I'm not distracting you with kisses to get information out of you." He pressed her into the wall, his body hardening again against her softness. "Your kisses are distracting me from my questions."

Capturing her lips with his, he kissed her hard before pulling away just long enough to tell her, "I was about to come in my pants, and was just trying to distract myself." He kissed the soft corner of her mouth and the tip of her nose. "I don't really give a shit if you don't tell me anything at all, just as long as you keep kissing me."

Her nipples tightened against his chest and moisture pooled between her thighs as he claimed her mouth again. His beard was soft against her chin and Heather moaned, her hands grasping his sides of their own accord. They slid underneath his shirt, up the firm slabs of muscle and across the light dusting of hair on his chest to grip his shoulders. He was so warm…and hard.

His hands dropped from the wall to grip her ass, squeezing hard. One leg wedged itself between hers until she was riding his muscular thigh, which she did with abandon. She couldn't help it. She'd always been a lusty girl, and this male brought her to entire new levels of shamelessness. A low growl of approval rumbled through his chest, and he pulled her hips toward him. She could feel the warmth of his hands through her yoga pants, and she would've given anything at that moment to have them on her bare skin.

No sooner had the thought crossed her mind than his

hands slid up to her waistband. One of them slid up her back, underneath her shirt, while the other made its way under her pants and panties to cup a bare cheek in his large palm.

She broke off the kiss. "Brock…"

He stilled immediately. With a last squeeze and a groan of disappointment, he removed his hands from underneath her clothes. "Too fast? I'm sorry." Holding her hips, he pressed his forehead to hers, breathing as hard as she was.

"I just…" She stopped. She just what? Wanted him to stop? Wanted him to rip her clothes off and take her against the rough wall?

Wanted him to know who she was before they took it any further.

She opened her mouth to tell him when she felt him stiffen against her, and not in a good way. He lifted his head and stared toward the entrance. She could practically see his hackles rising.

"What is it?" she whispered.

He released her hips and stepped away, holding one finger to his lips, and then turned to face the entrance to the cave.

Her muscles tensed as her eyes flickered back between him and the entrance, waiting for a cue as to whether she should find a weapon of some sort and prepare to fight, or if she should get ready to run.

Tilting his head up, he sniffed the air. "Stay here," he ordered in a low tone that brooked no argument. His heavy boots made no sound at all as he silently slipped from the cave.

She did exactly as she'd been told for almost an entire ten seconds before she crept over to the entrance and peered out into the mist. Brock was nowhere to be seen, but she knew better than to call out and give away her presence there. She wasn't stupid.

As quietly as she could, she tiptoed along the right side of the small mound of earth that enclosed her hideout. Reaching the edge, she put her hands down on the damp moss that covered it and leaned over as far as she could, trying to see through the damn fog. But all she could see were the ghostly tree trunks that peppered the landscape around her hideout. Nothing moved. No birds sang. Nothing scampered through the tree limbs. All was quiet. Too quiet. It was downright unnerving.

She'd decided to go back toward the cave when her toe nudged something on the ground. She picked up Brock's shirt and pants and, looking around, found his boots.

If she'd found his clothes, that meant he was out here somewhere in wolf form. He could be miles away by now. She should definitely go back into the cave, but she felt too trapped in there. If someone or something other than Brock found her, there would be nowhere for her to run. Nowhere for her to hide.

But she could at least go stand by the entrance. That was fair, right? He hadn't actually told her to stay *inside* the cave.

She'd barely taken two steps when something cold and wet touched the back of her neck through the strands of her hair and a warm snuffle of breath lifted the goose flesh there. She froze in fear, a scream catching in her throat just as a large wolf-like thing with sun-kissed fur stepped up alongside her. His back was nearly up to her ribcage, and his large head was tilted toward her, not quite wolf - not quite human, his scathing blue eyes reprimanding her more severely than words ever could.

Heather gave him a sheepish shrug and a nervous smile, whispering, "I was just on my way back there. I swear!"

The wolf narrowed its eyes at her and tossed its head toward the stream, then trotted off in that direction. Was she supposed to follow him?

He stopped about twenty feet away and swung his head around to stare at her. She could still feel his anger because she hadn't followed his orders, but apparently he wasn't angry enough to abandon her to her fate.

She headed his way and he waited until she had caught up to him before he turned away and headed toward the creek. Tucking his clothes and his boots under one arm, she ran her fingers through a hunk of fur on the side of his neck and hung on tight, taking comfort in the feel of him as they walked together.

His eyes closed briefly at her touch, and a shiver rippled across his skin. She noticed his reaction, but didn't let go. She needed the reassurance.

"Is there something out here?" she asked quietly.

Giving her a sideways look, he gave his head a quick shake, but then growled low in his throat. She took that to mean that he felt like there was, but hadn't found anything yet.

He picked up their pace, discouraging any more questions. Heather struggled to keep up without tripping over the rocks and branches that littered the ground, but she didn't complain. She was just grateful to be with him and that he hadn't left her back in the cave to cower alone in the corner until he came back.

When they came alongside the stream he walked to the edge and then turned to follow it upstream. His ears swiveled around this way and that, twitching at every little noise, and she didn't need to be told to be as silent as possible. His body language was telling her that whatever threat he sensed was still out there.

She tried reaching out with her own untrained senses, but other than his rapidly diminishing anger with her, she felt nothing else. Nothing unusual. Blowing her hair out of her eyes on a frustrated exhale, she tried again. But still, nothing. His instincts alone were going to have to be enough to guide them.

They'd gone about a half-mile when he skidded to a halt. She stood next to him, breathing hard for a few seconds before she noticed he was staring at something. Glancing around the area first, she stepped closer and saw something glinting among the rocks at the edge of the water. Bending down, she reached into the icy water and picked it up. Her stomach clenched when she saw what it was.

A golden coin.

She dropped it back on the ground, intending to leave it there and keep on walking, but Brock nudged it closer to her again with his nose.

Frowning at him, she said, "No. I'm not playing his stupid game."

He shook his head up and down and pushed the coin right up to her foot. Heather sighed and picked it up again, sticking it in her coat pocket. "There. Now let's go."

After a brief hesitation, he joined her. They'd been walking for about five minutes when Heather asked, "Why does it seem like we've been passing that same exact fallen tree over and over again?" She glanced over at Brock, and his eyes were narrowed on the same tree she was talking about. So, he'd noticed it too.

He stopped and dug at the ground with his front paw. When he was finished, there was a distinct "H" dug into the dirt. Glancing over at her, he only started walking again after making sure she'd seen it.

A minute later, Heather saw that same fallen tree, and watching the ground in front of her, she wasn't surprised to see the form of an "H" dug into the ground. They stopped again. Looking behind them and then ahead of them, she asked him, "How is this possible? We can't be walking in circles. We're following the stream! We didn't cross it…" Unless the stream just went around in a circle and reconnected to itself? "Does the stream go in circles?"

He snuffled and shook his head.

"Then why do we keep coming back around to the same place?" she asked.

Brock shook himself, then sat down on his haunches and stared at her.

"What?" she snapped. She hadn't meant to sound like that, but she was frustrated and tired and she wanted to go home.

His eyes went purposely to her pocket, then to her hand, and back up to her face.

Heather shook her head, "Oh, hell no. I am NOT tossing this thing."

He cocked his head and stared at her, an infinity of patience in his gaze.

"I said no," she told him adamantly.

He huffed out a breath and gazed off into the distance. Waiting.

"Brock, we should try to keep going."

Other than one ear twitching toward the sound of her voice, he gave no indication that he had heard her.

"This coin is not the reason we can't leave where we are." But deep down inside, she knew that it could be exactly for that reason.

Rubbing her forehead with her fingertips, she sighed. "Fine. I'll throw the damn coin." With a feeling of dread, she pulled it from her pocket. Brock watched with anxious eyes as she flipped it into the air and called out, "Tails!" Catching it and flipping it over onto the back of her opposite hand, they both peered at it.

The narrow face of the Fae prince stared back at them.

"Well, hell," Heather breathed nervously.

Brock's blue eyes shot to her face, and then he jumped to his feet and began scanning the area around them. Shoving the coin back into her pocket, she slid her fingers through the hair on the back of his neck again and did the same, hanging on tight. Just in case. She had no idea what to expect. All she knew was that they had just lost the coin toss, and if winning one got them sucked into another world with no supplies or shelter to survive, the gods only knew what was about to happen now.

Suddenly he spun around in front of her so fast, he

didn't give her a chance to let go of his fur and a hunk of it came away in her fingers. A growl rumbled deep within his throat as he zeroed in on a single point in the distance. She peered through the fog, but try as she might, she couldn't see or hear anything.

His head suddenly whipped over to the left, and the hackles on the back of his neck stood up so high they formed a ragged mohawk from his head to his rump. He leaned against her, stepping sideways as he pushed her back toward the water, his eyes intently studying the trees.

Heather got his drift and stumbled back to the creek until she was standing at the edge of the water. He took up a protective position in front of her and bared his teeth in warning, his eyes shifting back and forth. Lowering his head and chest, his snarls ripped through the air, accompanied by snaps of his teeth as he made his claim on her known.

She backed up some more until the icy water was lapping at her sneakers and drenching the already damp hem of her yoga pants. Sweat beaded on her upper lip as she desperately tried to see through the damn fog, but try as she might, she couldn't see what was coming for them.

But something was coming, that much was sure. And it wasn't anything they'd be happy to see. She could feel its menacing presence weighing on the air around them.

They waited for what felt like an eternity. Heather tried to keep her breathing quiet, even though she really felt like screaming, just to break the tension. She still couldn't see anything, but she could hear it now: Puffs of breath in front of them and to the left. Branches and dried-up pine needles broke under heavy footsteps that came steadily closer. Whatever it was, it sounded large. The cloying smell of rotten meat hung heavy in the damp, cool air, becoming stronger with every passing second. Her stomach heaved and she tried breathing through her mouth, but it only made it worse.

Brock paced back and forth in front of her nervously a few times, and then stopped and held his ground. Head lowered, teeth bared, eyes glowing with a preternatural light, he watched and waited.

She wiped her clammy palms on his clothes and hugged them to her chest. This was so not going to be good. She could sense that much at least. Her heart was racing, and her blood was roaring through her veins at such a speed that her vision was beginning to darken at the corners. Taking a deep breath, she willed herself to calm down.

Brock's head dropped lower still, until his chin nearly touched the ground, and more vicious snarls ripped from his throat one on top of the other until chills broke out on her skin. He stared hard straight ahead, every muscle in his wolf-like body tensed and ready.

The mist stirred in front of them, breaking apart like wisps of a cloud. Heather caught a glance of a yellow eye narrowed at Brock. It was surrounded by muted green leather skin and black stripes. As it came closer, a large head with rows of sharp teeth revealed itself, and then swung around to its right. She followed its gaze to find an identical pair of yellow eyes pinned on her.

Raptors? Velociraptors? How could that be? Heather's blood pulsed as her heart started pumping in triple time.

She was both fascinated and terrified of dinosaurs. Ever since she saw the first Jurassic Park movie. Thank God there was no way in hell those things still existed.

Except here they were.

The one directly ahead advanced on them, and Heather saw that she had, in fact, been mistaken. They weren't quite velociraptors. They were something much worse. For one, velociraptors didn't have black claws the length of a T-Rex's dripping with some type of fluid. They also didn't shriek like a banshee, or have stiff spines covering their wrinkly, dark skin from the neck down. And they didn't have six-inch long teeth, set in double rows in their wide, open mouths.

But velociraptors *would* use those powerful back legs to cover a good twenty feet of open ground with one leap to land directly in front of her werewolf.

Brock reared up on his hind legs, coming face to face with the creature, and then dove forward, slashing out with his enormous paws and going for its throat. But the thing knocked him aside with one short arm like the giant werewolf was naught but a teacup Chihuahua.

Its gaze immediately locked in on Heather. She had to stiffen her knees to keep her legs from buckling underneath her as the thing tilted its head, its intelligent eyes searching her face. For what, she couldn't begin to guess.

It took a step toward her and Brock's clothes tumbled out of her arms to land in the muck at her feet as her blood turned to ice. She wanted to run, but she couldn't force herself to move. She wanted to do something to help Brock. She wanted to close her eyes and open them again to discover that she'd only been having a bad dream.

It took another step just as Brock let out a roar, the pure savagery of the sound finally jolted into action. Remembering her kickboxing training (one of the things that she did trying to win the constant battle with her weight) she kicked out with her most powerful front kick, catching it in the stomach with the ball of her foot. It kept coming. Hands up on each side of her head to protect her face, she ducked low and swung her right fist upwards in an uppercut, landing it square in the vicinity of where its kidney should be. Then she stepped back and followed it up with a perfect roundhouse kick, the top of her foot making a satisfying thud as it connected.

It didn't seem to affect it at all. It just kept coming. She stumbled back farther into the stream. The icy water streamed over and into her shoes, making her bones ache.

Lots of good all of those damned classes did.

Razor-like, pointed claws lifted toward her face, dripping with that strange fluid, but it barely registered. Her body flashed hot and cold, a whimper escaping her as she waited for those talons to slice into her face.

Eyes wide, she stared up at the thing. It almost appeared to be smiling at her, an evil glint in its yellow eyes, and a scream tore from her throat. She squeezed her eyes closed as the claws flashed toward her face. Raising her arms to protect herself as best she could, she waited for the pain, but it never came.

Opening her eyes again, she saw the reason why. Brock was on top of the creature, his massive paws digging into its upper arms as his teeth snapped at the thing's jugular. The spines on its back were embedded deep into the ground, stuck like spikes and hampering its movements.

A motion caught out of the corner of her eye tore her attention away from the match in front of her. The second creature came flying through the air, straight into Brock. Its momentum carried them both away from the first creature, and they rolled over and over, caught in a gruesome hug, landing half in and half out of the stream.

The other one, still stuck in the ground, began rocking back and forth on its back, loosening the dirt around its spines.

Heather's body finally caught up with her mind and she spun around, looking for a weapon. Finding a rock that looked big enough, she hefted it in her palm to feel its weight, then hauled back and threw it as hard as she could at the thing's head. It hit it right above its right eye, leaving an ugly gash. Screaming with rage, the thing renewed its efforts to get free, and this time managed to make some serious headway.

Shit. All she'd managed to do was piss it off.

As it rolled onto one side and then the other, she turned and ran, splashing through the creek to the other side. She fell up the opposite bank, scraping her hands and knees on the rocks, but she barely flinched, scrambling to her feet and turning around to see what was happening.

Brock was caught underneath the heavier body of the dinosaur that had tackled him. As she watched in horror, it sank its teeth into his shoulder. Brock howled and roared in anger and pain and lifted his back legs, kicking the thing off of him and rolling away. It took a mouthful of his flesh and muscle with it.

They both landed on their feet and faced off, circling each other slowly on their hind legs in a macabre dance. Brock's sapphire eyes were glowing with an unholy light, and his teeth were bared in a bloody semblance of a snarl. Heather saw black liquid dripping down the creature's neck where he'd bitten it, and hoped it was blood.

The first creature finally freed itself from the ground and flipped over with help from its long tail, pushing itself up to a standing position. It glanced over at her, then turned its attention to the fight going on downstream. With one powerful leap, it landed directly behind Brock.

"Behind you!" she screamed, just as it lunged at him with both arms outstretched.

Brock fell to all fours, twisting out of the way just in time. The thing's momentum kept it going and it fell toward the other one, unable to stop itself. It pulled its arms back to avoid its friend, but not quick enough.

The second creature shrieked in pain as its chest was flayed wide open by the other's claws. More black liquid gushed from the new wounds, joining the river that was running from its neck. It fell down onto all fours, its head bouncing loosely on its neck, then it toppled over onto its side.

And then there was one.

Without giving it time to react, Brock flew toward it and caught one of its front legs in his powerful jaws as he knocked it off balance. It toppled over backwards, and he landed on top of it, his weight again spearing the thing's spines into the ground. It shrieked and hissed in frustration, its teeth snapping within inches of Brock's head. Those long canines came perilously close before he jerked his head back, still holding its arm in his jaws. It swung its other arm at him, but he blocked it and slammed it into the ground with his front paw.

Brock's muscles strained as he adjusted his bite closer to its hand, and his back feet dug into the dirt as he pressed forward with everything he had. The creature struggled against him, its yellow eyes rolling back in its head as it fought against Brock's hold.

Heather stood silent and unmoving as she watched their battle of wills, afraid of distracting Brock and causing him to lose his grip.

A deep growl rose from Brock's chest and he jerked forward with a surge of strength. At the same time, the creature wiggled its other arm out and raised it to strike at Brock's neck, claws dripping that fatal fluid.

A flash of fear and anger ripped through Heather. Without realizing she had moved at all, she was back across the stream with a breath of the air. It had taken her less than a heartbeat. Not stopping to think about it, she raised her right hand toward the thing. Blue-white bolts of heat left her fingers, hitting the creature directly in the ribcage right where its heart should be. The body jerked, the arm that had been poised over the werewolf flung back onto the ground as the volts of electricity shot through its body. Eyes glowing white from the kick of power traveling within his prey, Brock surged forward once more, pushing its arm in toward itself and slicing the thing open with its own claws.

Releasing the arm, he jumped back away from it. His sides heaved and his eyes struggled to stay open as he recovered from the shock he'd just received, watching the raptor carefully for any signs of life.

But he needn't have bothered. Whether from Heather's lightening bolt or the poison claws, or both, the thing was dead.

Brock staggered over to it and nudged it with his nose, then nipped at its leg. It didn't move. Backing away, he gave her a mistrustful look (that honestly she took offense at being that she'd just saved his mangy life) and collapsed onto his haunches. She could see his muscles quivering with exhaustion from where she stood.

Heather heard a loud snap echo around them, like a large branch breaking in two. Brock threw his head back and howled as his spine twisted and his upper torso jerked forward and back. The howl turned into a human roar of pain as she heard more cracks and pops, his body bending in angles that should not be possible, his limbs breaking and reforming. She covered her ears from the sounds as his snout and teeth retracted and his skin rippled over his tearing muscles, changing…reforming, until he was once again a human male.

Naked, his shoulder bleeding from the gaping wound inflicted on it during the fight, he collapsed onto his side in the dirt.

Heather picked her way carefully back over to the stream where she'd dropped his things earlier. It wouldn't help anything if she fell and bashed her head open on one of these rocks. Picking up his clothes and bringing them back to where he lay, she covered his bare ass (a bit reluctantly) with his shirt before she made her way around to the front of him.

He watched her as she kneeled down in front of him, his blue eyes wary and dark with exhaustion. His shoulder was bloody and dirty, and already beginning to heal. She needed to get it clean. As she went to stand up again, his hand shot out and wrapped around her wrist with surprising strength.

"What th' fook was that?" he rasped.

She cocked an eyebrow at the new accent, but decided not to argue the point that now was hardly the time to try to distract her with a sexy, Scottish brogue. Besides, she kinda liked it. "What was what?" she asked innocently. Then she shushed him when he opened his mouth to clarify the question. "We need to get your shoulder taken care of. Stay here." Before he could ask anything else, she got up and went foraging through the undergrowth around the trees. Finding what she was looking for, she plucked off some leaves and took them over to him.

He managed to sit up by himself with hardly a grunt of pain when she returned. The shirt she'd kinda sorta covered him with slid down his hard abs to pool around his lean hips, and Heather had to bite down hard on the inside of her cheek to stay focused on what she was doing.

She kneeled down next to him and pulled his hair away from the sticky wound. Normally she wasn't a fan of long hair on guys, but on him, it worked. A little too well. Maybe it was because the rest of him was so masculine.

Wiping away the dirt as best as she could, she packed his wound with the leaves. He gritted his teeth when she pushed them in there, but otherwise showed no sign of the discomfort he was in.

"What is that?" he hissed out when she hit a particularly tender spot.

She glanced up at him, but he was looking off into the distance. "Um, I think it's called Lamb's Ear?"

He tensed as she pressed her hand over the leaves, applying pressure. "You think that's what it is? What if yer sockin' me full of poison sumac or something?"

"It's not poison sumac," she said distractedly. "My mom used to use this on me all the time as a kid. Mostly for smaller scrapes and cuts. I just don't recall the name."

He grunted in response, but said nothing else.

She, on the other hand, was trying really, really hard to keep her eyes on his shoulder. But they kept wandering down that sculpted torso of his of their own accord. Luckily, he didn't seem to be paying attention, distracted as he was by her pressing on his injury.

"I don't see any signs of poisoning," she muttered more to herself than to him.

He glanced back at the creature that had taken the chunk out of him. "I don't think their teeth were venomous. Just their claws."

After a long moment, she said, "So. That shape shifting stuff. It doesn't look fun."

He'd closed his eyes, but opened them again at her words, finally looking at her as he admitted, "It's not."

Careful to keep her face neutral, she nodded, not sure what else to say. "Here, hold these." She replaced her hand with his over the leaves. "Be right back." Getting up, she went to the water to wet a piece of her shirt so she could wipe off the remaining blood. "Why not just stay in one shape or the other then?" she asked when she returned.

"Well, for one, I don't always have a choice."

She lifted an eyebrow in question and continued wiping off his shoulder and arm with one hand while the other took over the compression.

He winced when she pressed a little too hard, and reaching up, pushed her hands away. "That's good enough. Thank you."

"But you need to keep pressure on…"

"Yeah, I got it."

She tried not to feel hurt by his brusque tone. Males were always grumpy when they weren't feeling good. "You gonna be ok?"

"It'll be fine by tomorrow."

She got to her feet and backed off, turning around as he started to get up. His pants cracked behind her as he tried to shake the mud off of them.

"Sorry about the muck on your clothes."

He only grunted in answer and she scowled at the fog. He didn't need to be like that. It's not like she'd dropped them on purpose.

"All right, let's go."

Turning around, she found that he'd gotten his muddy pants and boots on and had wadded up his dirty shirt and was holding it as a compress on his shoulder.

"That shirt is dirty," she scolded.

"Don't worry, the leaves are still there. Even though they're probably infecting me more than the dirt would have."

He walked away without looking at her again, heading upstream.

Males could be so moody.

CHAPTER 9

Brock's gut churned with unease as he led the way in front of Heather. He was almost positive he'd seen blue lights come from her fingertips to zap that thing right before he'd sliced it open with its own claws. But that was impossible. Wasn't it?

Because she was human.

So then, how had she traveled back across the stream so fast she'd been invisible to the naked eye? Just appearing right next to him all of a sudden?

Maybe the fog had played tricks with his eyesight. He glanced back over his shoulder and then quickly forward again, not wanting her to catch him staring. But her head was down, her brow furrowed as she concentrated on watching where she was walking so she wouldn't trip.

And what was with the fighting skills? He'd seen her kicking and punching like a pro, her usual adorable clumsiness curiously gone. He glanced back again, studying her a bit longer this time. He didn't know what he was looking for, just…something. Something that would give him a clue as to whether he was correct in what he thought he'd seen, or proof that he was indeed losing his mind in this place.

"Go ahead," she said from behind him after he'd turned back around for the second time. "Ask."

He didn't break stride or show any other sign that he was surprised she had caught him ogling her. "Ask what?"

"I can see the smoke coming out of your ears from here. Just ask me. Before you hurt your brain cells."

This time when he looked back he found her eyes on him as they walked, her expression resigned. He just gave her a small shake of his head, not sure he really wanted to know. As he was about to face forward again, she tripped on a branch lying across the ground. Arms flailing, she reached out for him and he caught her by the elbows, lifting her up and over the branch and setting her firmly on her feet.

"Thanks," she murmured, still hanging onto his arms.

He was surprised to see a slight blush blossom across her face. Heather? Embarrassed?

She peeped up at him through her lashes. "Not the most graceful person in the world, am I?"

No, she wasn't. Unless, of course, she was skipping around from place to place like a ghost or something. Or launching ninja kicks at an extinct creature that shouldn't even be around anymore. He frantically searched for something to say that wouldn't sound like he found her clumsiness anything less than endearing when she suddenly grinned at him, laughing at herself, and butterflies fluttered in his stomach like he was a boy of fourteen again.

It took him a moment before he could find his voice. "The ground here isn't very level, and there's a lot of debris. You need to watch where you're going." He sounded overly stern even to his own ears.

Her grin faded as quickly as it had appeared. "Thanks, Captain Obvious. I'll strive to be more careful."

She let go of his arms, and he looked down at where she'd been touching him, frowning at himself, only to see his skin streaked with blood. Happy for the distraction from his previous thoughts, he grabbed her wrists and flipped her hands over. The skin of both of her palms was torn and bloodied, the cuts filled with dirt and little rocks. How had he not noticed her hands when she'd been tending to him earlier? He redirected his frown to her and she rolled her eyes, yanking her arms out of his grasp.

"I'm fine. And in my defense, I was running from a raptorsaurus thing that was coming after me with those long claws. A situation in which anyone could have tripped and skinned their hands and knees."

He immediately dropped his eyes to her torn pants and crouched down on his haunches in front of her. Ignoring her protests, he held her still with one large hand wrapped around the back of her upper thigh and tugged up her wet pant leg with the other. Sure enough, her knee was in the same shape as her hands. And by the looks of the holes in her other pant leg, so was her other one.

Releasing her shapely leg with a twinge of remorse, he told her, "We need to get these scrapes washed off, before they get infected."

She glanced over at the icy stream. "I'd rather just keep walking." Her eyes skittered around nervously, even though it was impossible to see anything coming through the fog. "There might be more of those things."

"There's not," he assured her.

"How do you know?"

"Because they stink like they've been rotting in the ground for millions of years, which they have. I can smell them a mile away. And I don't smell anything right now except for those two." He pointed with his chin at the two dead ones lying downstream.

"Guess they do have a kind of unique stench," she agreed, but her forehead was still wrinkled up with worry.

Taking pity on her, he acquiesced. "All right. We'll follow the stream until we find somewhere to bunker down for the night, then I'll get a fire going and find some food."

She nodded her approval. "Sounds good to me. Let's go." Taking the lead this time, she started following the stream back the way they had come.

Wondering how in the world she'd ever managed to survive this long in life, he called out with a touch of amusement, "Heather."

Glancing back over her shoulder to see him still standing right where she'd left him, she waved him forward impatiently.

"Heather!"

Finally, she stopped. "What?" she snapped.

"You're going the wrong way. We need to go upstream, not down."

Turning on her heel without another word, she

stomped back in his direction. As she passed him, she grumbled, "Are you just going to stand here all day? Let's go."

He gave her a lopsided grin. "Yes, ma'am." Females could be so moody.

HE FOLLOWED behind her in relative silence for a few more hours. They hadn't run across anything else except for a skoochat that had been startled from his hiding place as they passed. Brock had managed to catch it in his current human form when it ran into a hole, not wanting to damage his healing shoulder by changing again. Their dinner now swung lifeless from his hand at his side along with his shirt. His wound had long since stopped bleeding.

Heather had been unusually pensive since he'd caught it. And by the looks she was giving its limp body, he would bet that she was busy thinking up new excuses not to eat it.

He let her stew about it as they trekked on, caught up in his own thoughts for the most part anyway. And when he wasn't mulling over this whole situation he'd somehow found himself in, he'd been quite happily distracted by the view of her plump behind twitching from side to side in front of him as she walked. Her backside was a thing of mouth-watering beauty, the yoga pants she was wearing doing absolutely nothing to hide her lush curves, and it reminded him of the plans he'd had before all of this had happened.

The naked plans.

They could talk about her sprinting and Taser talents later. For now, he pushed those thoughts to the farthest recesses of his mind, not wanting them to ruin his appreciation of the view. His obsession with that luscious backside was also the reason that he noticed when she started limping.

"You okay up there?" he asked her.

Not lifting her eyes from the trail they were following, she mumbled, "Fine."

He narrowed his eyes at the back of her head. She wasn't fine. The fact that she'd even said it meant that she wasn't. Every male worth his salt knew that. Shoving his hair out of his face with one hand, he wished for the twentieth time that he had a hair band to tie the stuff back with. He watched her closely for a few more seconds.

Yeah, she was definitely limping, though she was trying hard to hide it.

He scoped out the area around them, looking for a good spot to camp for the night so she could rest. He'd just claim he wanted to stop because of his healing shoulder. But all he saw was the stream they were following to their right and more trees to their left. It was damn near impossible to see anything beyond that.

Increasing his steps to his normal pace, he caught up with her easily and took her by the hand. She jumped, startled at the touch, but didn't pull away. When she looked up at him, he could see the strain around her eyes. Could see the pain she was trying to hide. "Let's wander off the path a bit. Find somewhere with some shelter," he offered.

She nodded agreeably. Too agreeably. She must really be hurting.

He could easily carry her with very little effort on his part, but somehow he knew that wouldn't go over well. So, he slowed his pace again to accommodate her and let her hobble along next to him.

They'd gone about another two hundred feet when he thought he caught a whiff of sulfur. It wasn't strong, but it was there.

"Do you smell that?" he asked.

She took a whiff and wrinkled her nose. "Yeah. It smells like rotten eggs."

He grinned down at her. "It smells like a hot spring. Like nature's hot tub."

That definitely caught her interest, if the sudden spark of life in her eyes was any indication.

"A hot tub?" she asked, as though she couldn't quite believe that she had heard him correctly.

Brock laughed. "Come on!"

A few minutes later there was a break in the trees and suddenly there it was, nestled amongst the pines like something from a wet dream.

Brock released Heather's hand and walked up to the edge. The natural pool was bordered by rock and surrounded by grass and pine trees. Steam rose from the surface of the clear water to mingle with the ever-present mist. Bright colored stones glittered along the bottom. It looked deep enough to submerge even a male of his size, and it was wide enough to fit a good dozen people.

And they had it all to themselves.

Without another thought, he dropped the skoochat

and his shirt on the ground. He was kicking off his boots and his hands were at the waistband of his pants when Heather coughed uncomfortably.

"What are you doing?"

"I'm getting in," he told her matter of factly. He couldn't wait to feel that hot water washing away the grime and soothing his tired, sore muscles. "I suggest you do the same."

She opened her mouth, looking as if she was about to protest, but glanced over at the water and snapped it shut again. Yanking off her running jacket, she dropped it on top of his shirt.

"Thatta girl." He smiled with encouragement and yanked off his pants. Naked as the day he was born, he stepped up onto the rocks and searched for a way to ease himself in. He didn't want to jump only to find out the water was too hot, or worse, not water at all in this freaky place. Finding a ledge about a foot under the water and a little to his left, he stepped down, waited a few seconds to make sure it was safe, and then lowered himself into the hot water with a blissful groan. It was the perfect temperature for a bath.

Leaning back and closing his eyes, he moaned again as the hot minerals began to work their way into his tired muscles. He listened for the sounds of Heather joining him and wondered if his imagination would do the naked reality of her any justice. However, when the telltale rustling of clothing being removed didn't come, he frowned at the deafening silence and opened his eyes to find Heather staring at him in something akin to shock.

She stood frozen with her shirt halfway off, one arm

out of its sleeve, her expressive eyes wide and unblinking and glued to his bare chest. He cocked an eyebrow at her, pleased that his bare form had incited such a reaction as he waited for her to return the favor. When she finally noticed him watching her, she blinked a few times, coming out of her daze. And then she frowned.

"Turn around," she ordered.

But he just lifted his arms back up onto the rocks beside him and settled in to enjoy the show. "No way," he told her with a shake of his head. "You've gotten to ogle me shamelessly a few times now. It's my turn."

She looked from him to the water and back to him again, chewing the inside of her cheek.

"Come on, sunshine. The water's fine." He splashed some of it at her, and after a deep breath, she pulled her other arm out and lifted her shirt up and off.

His cock, already feeling frisky from watching her strutting around in front of him all day, came to immediate attention at the sight of her full breasts spilling from the top of her peach colored bra. When she leaned over to untie her sneakers, he held his breath, praying that the silky material would give way from (what had to be) the tremendous weight of them. But alas, it did not. He didn't even attempt to hide his disappointment as she stood back up. Luckily, she refused to look at him and so she didn't notice. If she had, she might have been too self-conscious to continue.

Kicking off her shoes, she hooked her thumbs under the waistband of her pants and slid them down her curvy hips, revealing matching panties and smooth, rounded thighs that tapered down to shapely calves and delicate ankles and feet. Keeping her face hidden behind her hair, she carefully waded into the pool still wearing her barely-there underwear.

He bit his bottom lip and gripped the rocks under his hands in an attempt to keep himself in his seat.

As she stepped down onto the rocky ledge, he noticed the large, broken blisters on the backs of her heels and knew that's why she'd been limping. And she hadn't complained or said a word the entire time. Maybe she was tougher than he'd given her credit for.

"They could've dropped a toothbrush and some soap with those clothes you're wearing," she grumbled. "And maybe some spare clothes. And a bed. A bed would be freakin' nice. A soft, thick bed."

Brock bit back a smile. He'd spoken too soon.

She let out a hiss as she sat down and submersed her skinned knees and hands into the hot water.

He slid off the ledge and moved to stand in front of her. As he'd predicted, the water was so deep it nearly came up to his shoulders. "Here, let me see." Trying not to stare at the enticing sight of her wet, and now nearly see-thru, bra, he took one of her hands in his. Gently, he brushed at the scrapes, removing the dirt and grime. He did the same with her other hand, and then slid his hand under her leg to lift her knee up and work on those.

Neither of them spoke while he tended to her, though he could hear her heart pounding as hard as his was. Both of them overly aware of their undressed state in this close proximity.

Once her wounds were cleaned, he set her leg back down onto the ledge, but didn't remove his hand. Instead, he slid it up along the outside of her thigh until he reached her hip. He squeezed, feeling her supple flesh and the muscle underneath, before running his thumb over the top of her leg to tease at the edge of her panties. She stopped breathing completely, but didn't protest, and he lifted his eyes to her face to check her reaction.

Her cheeks were flushed, whether from the water or from what he was doing, he didn't know. As he watched, her tongue darted out to moisten her parted lips.

He was instantly and irrationally jealous of that tongue for getting to taste her.

Giving her time to stop him if she so wished, he moved his free hand to her other leg, mimicking the movements of the first, both thumbs sliding just under the edge of her panties to feel the crease where her legs met her woman-hood. Her eyes darkened and her chest rose and fell with her heavy breaths, the water lapping at her breasts, teasing him as it got her bra a little wetter every time.

His eyes fell to those luscious breasts, then lower under the water to her stomach and plump hips. He stepped in closer, his heart pounding, and she spread her legs wide to accommodate him. She lifted her hands and gripped his biceps, and a deep growl rumbled in his chest even at that innocent touch.

"What about your shoulder?" she whispered. "We should wash it out."

"Later," he insisted. Lowering his head, he captured her pretty mouth with his. He kissed her gently at first, savoring her taste, but when she moaned in his mouth, he lost any semblance of self-control.

One hand tightened on her hip while the other lifted

to cup the back of her head. Wrapping her long, chestnut hair around his fist, he held her still as he kissed her with all of the pent up passion he'd been feeling since they'd left the cave.

Her fingers burrowed into his hair, holding it back from his face as she returned his kisses with the same abandon that she seemed to do everything in life, her tongue dueling with his and her little teeth nipping at his lips until he thought he would go insane if he didn't get inside of her.

Releasing her head, he lifted her off of the ledge and slid her down his body, wrapping her legs around his narrow hips. Her arms tightened around his neck, landing on his shoulder wound, but he was too jazzed up to feel it. The blood rushed through his veins and his cock got impossibly harder at the feel of so much pure woman wrapped around him.

"Heather," he breathed against her ear. "I need tae be inside of you. Please..."

"Yes," she answered after a slight hesitation. "Brock. Yes..."

He kissed her again while he unhooked her bra, and she leaned back just enough to slide it down her arms and off, leaving it to float in the water next to them. With her still wrapped around him, he held her to him with one arm around her back and used the other to help lift them both out of the water and out onto the soft grass. The smell of the earth mixed with her natural blossom scent. It surrounded him like the mist in the air, engulfing him in her passion.

Clad in nothing but her panties, she reached up and

tried to pull him down on top of her. But he'd waited for what felt like forever to see her like this, and he wasn't about to miss this chance. Kissing her soundly, he captured both her wrists in one hand and placed them over her head, holding them there. "I want tae see you."

She tried to break his hold. "Brock, what are you doing?" But when she saw the stubborn gleam in his eye, she stilled underneath him, her chest heaving and her eyes unsure.

Kissing her cheek, he kept her arms above her head and rolled off to the side. His heart stalled in his chest even as his blood pulsed and his groin tightened at the sight of her spread out before him like a luscious buffet. She was even hotter than he'd imagined. And not because of the water.

Soft, rounded breasts were crowned with dusky areolas. Water dripped from his hair onto her nipples and they stiffened prettily as he watched. He licked his lips and her back arched, encouraging him to taste them, but he wasn't done yet.

He lowered his gaze to her soft belly, past the freckle next to her navel, and on down to the sweet curve of her hips and the shadow of the dark curls under her wet panties.

She squirmed underneath his gaze, pressing her thighs together. "Brock…"

Her voice was thick with need, and he couldn't deny her (or himself) anymore. Lowering his head, he flicked her nipple with his tongue, rolling it around before sucking it into his mouth and nipping it with his teeth.

She bucked underneath him and tried to roll toward him, but he pressed her back with a hand on her hip.

Still holding her wrists with one hand, he released her hip and cupped her other breast with the other. It overflowed his fingers as he kneaded her before gently pinching her nipple, and she cried out, her body surging upward again to get closer to him.

Throwing one heavy leg over hers, he worked his thigh between them, opening her to his touch. Nipping at the underside of her breast, he ran his hand down her belly to cup her through her panties. Her hips bucked and his cock twitched in response, reaching for her heat. He ground himself into her hip, seeking some relief as he teased her with his fingers and suckled at her breast.

She made a sound of protest when he lifted his hand from her, only to moan with pleasure when he slid it underneath the material to touch her bare skin. His fingers quickly found the source of her pleasure within her damp folds, and he raised his head to watch her face as he brought her to the edge and beyond.

Her eyes closed and she stiffened beneath him as she pressed herself against his palm until with a cry, she came hard, her body jerking uncontrollably with the force of it.

Brock growled with need at the sight. Releasing her wrists, he sat up and yanked her panties down her legs. Her plump thighs cradled his hips as he lowered himself on top of her and found her opening with the tip of his cock. With one powerful surge he entered her. She was hot and wet and gripped him so tight he began to shake, losing what little control he'd managed to retain up until this point.

He wanted to take his time. Wanted to enjoy the feel of her thoroughly. But his body had a mind of its own. Her arms and legs wrapped around him as he began to move in and out, his strokes hard and fast, until with a roar, he exploded inside of her sweet warmth.

Spent, his head dropped onto her shoulder as he continued to slide in and out, slower now, as they both caught their breath. He felt her hands rubbing his back, and his heart ached in his chest even as his cock swelled within her once again.

He groaned, both with need and with despair.

CHAPTER 10

Brock was crushing her, but Heather didn't care. Breathing was overrated, as far as she was concerned. And if she died, well, she couldn't think of a more perfect way to go than being smothered by this beautiful male as he loved her.

She felt him stirring inside of her again and her muscles clenched around him in response. His moan mixed with hers as he started to move inside of her again with long, sure strokes.

He lifted his weight up onto his elbows and she took a deep breath. His beautiful hair fell around them like a curtain as he gazed down at her face, his blue eyes so intense she began to get a bit uncomfortable. But when she closed her eyes, he nipped at her bottom lip.

"Open yer eyes, sunshine. Look at me."

She did, and he held her captive with his gaze as he increased his pace within her until she cried out from the intensity of it.

"I can't get enough of ye," he breathed. Then he pulled back and slammed into her hard. Her hands gripped his tight ass, encouraging him to do it again.

He did, over and over. Then he shifted his hips slightly and Heather's eyes drifted closed as she lost herself in the feelings he was invoking inside of her. Reaching between them, he slid his thumb over her clit as he pounded into her. She arched toward him, the pressure building higher and higher, until with a few final thrusts she shattered around him with an incoherent cry.

Throwing his head back, his voice joined hers and she felt him pulsing inside of her. Needing something to hang onto, she held him tight as he slowed his pace again, his body trembling as he brought them down. She sighed happily, tightening her arms around his muscular shoulders and pulling him down to her to hug him to her.

"I'm going to crush you," he grumbled in her ear, but he made no move to get up.

Not that she would have let him anyway. She wanted to stay in this moment just a little longer, before reality caught up to them again.

Her stomach chose that moment to growl loudly.

And there it was…

Brock did move then. "You're hungry. Let me get dinner going." With a kiss on the corner of her mouth, he carefully extracted himself and rolled off of her. Running a hand over her curves from her neck to her thigh, he gave her a squeeze and sighed with longing, then sat up and pulled her up with him. "Come on. I'll build a fire and we can wash our clothes. We'll dry them by the fire."

"And what am I supposed to wear while they're drying?" she asked with a quirk of her brow.

He gave her a naughty grin, got to his feet, and offered her a hand, completely unabashed by his own nudity.

Of course if she had a body like that, she'd run around naked all the time too.

Taking his hand, she followed him back into the natural spring, trying to stay behind him so he wouldn't notice all of her jiggly bits.

* * *

A FEW HOURS LATER, they were lying naked in the grass with her back snuggled up against his front. His arm was wrapped tightly around her middle, and between that and the fire in front of her, she was snug as a bug in spite of the oncoming night and the dropping temperature.

Their clothes were washed and strewn across the grass on the other side of the flames, and they themselves had had more than one dip in the spring as Brock had insisted on washing her after each time he'd lifted her from the water to have his way with her. A "way" she'd fully encouraged. And at least she'd managed to get his shoulder wound clean somewhere in there. It looked to be healing nicely.

She sighed, knowing that eventually they were going to have to get around to talking. He had questions, she knew, and she would have to answer them honestly.

And the chances were pretty good that he would want nothing to do with her after he got those answers. But she wouldn't lie to him. Lies only got you into more trouble.

She sighed again. She would miss him.

"What's that about?" he asked between the feather light kisses he was dropping on the back of her shoulder.

She looked back at him with a sad smile. "Nothing," she lied. "Just wondering how much longer we're going to be stuck here."

He propped his chin on her shoulder and stared at the flames. His answering sigh matched hers. "Well, if we can avoid any more lost coin tosses, it shouldn't be more than a couple more days." He paused, and she thought he wasn't going to say anymore about it. Then he blurted, "That prince of yours, he sure has an interesting sense of humor. I mean, what's the deal with him? Sending us here? What's the point?"

"I have no idea," she answered honestly. But she supposed they would find out, eventually. When the prince was good and ready to tell them.

Why, out of all the places in the entire world, had her people decided to hide out in the bustling city of Seattle? "Stupid, freaking faeries," she mumbled out loud. Immediately, she slapped a hand over her mouth, hoping she'd caught the words before he'd heard them. But no such luck.

Brock stiffened behind her. And then she felt the cool night breeze against her bare back as he sat up to look down at her with a guarded expression. "Did you just say 'faeries'? Like, as in *Faeries*? Fae people? People of the forest? Evil, witch-like creatures that like tae fuck wit' everyone?"

There was that accent again, which she was quickly learning only came out when he was feeling very emotional. Dammit. Why couldn't she keep her mouth shut just for a few more hours?

Sitting up, she scooted over to her clothes. They were just about dry, thank the gods. She couldn't have this conversation naked.

Brock seemed to have no such qualms. Wrapping his arms around his bare knees, he sat in the grass and waited for her while she pulled on her tee shirt and panties.

Feeling slightly less vulnerable, she scratched her forehead, trying to think of a way to make her answer less shocking. Unfortunately, she didn't think she could.

He stared at her across the fire, his expression unreadable as he repeated, "Heather, did you say 'Faeries'?"

She heaved a heavy sigh and nodded. "I did."

"How do you know what they are?" he asked, his tone laced with suspicion.

Ah. The hundred-dollar question. She chewed her bottom lip while avoiding his eyes. She studied her healing palms. She peeked up at him through her lashes and dropped her eyes again. She ran her fingers through the long, tangled strands of her hair.

He sat still as a statue while she fidgeted. "Heather. How do you know?"

Hanging her head, she let her hair fall forward to cover her face, hiding behind it like the coward that she was. "Because I am one," she whispered.

Brock was silent for a long time. When he finally spoke, his deep voice was a full octave higher than normal. "I'm sorry?"

She lifted her head, cleared her throat, and spoke clearly this time. "Because I am one. I'm Fae." Let him judge her if he wanted to. She wasn't ashamed. She had no control over how she'd been born. She only had control over how she lived her life now that she was here. And thanks to her parents stealing her away when she was a child, she'd managed to do that as far removed from being a Fae as possible. In other words, she was a good person.

He blinked at her with shocked blue eyes for a good ten seconds. Dropping his gaze to her knees, he studied the rapidly healing flesh there. Then he rubbed the sides of his face with both hands, rifling the short hairs of his close-cropped beard and smoothing it down again. "So that explains the ghosting about, and the electricity shooting from your fingers." He laughed quietly in disbelief, showing straight, white teeth, then became deadly serious again as his eyes returned to her.

Heather sat quietly as he had earlier, waiting for him to take in the fact that he, a werewolf, had just had sex multiple times with her, a Faerie. Something that just wasn't done.

He pulled his hair back off of his face and rubbed his eyes. "I thought they were extinct."

"Not exactly. More like in hiding."

"And you. *You* are one o' those things?"

She nodded.

An epiphany came across his face. "Ah. I should have guessed from the moment I met you. That's why you smell so good."

"Like the flowers?"

"Yes. But, you're nothing like I was told to expect," he said as he studied her from across the fire like the bug she'd felt like a few minutes earlier. "For one, you haven't tried tae siphon my soul from my body yet, at least nae that I've noticed. Or is it only humans that are susceptible tae that?"

"I'm not that type of Fae," she said.

"What kind o' Fae are you then?" he asked. "Exactly?"

She could see his mind churning. Going over everything she'd said and done since he'd met her. She wished she could say something to ease it, but she was kind of at a loss herself. She'd been raised outside of the tribe, raised nearly identically to humans. She'd never tapped into her Fae self, until he'd almost died fighting those raptor things. Before today, she'd never known she could make electricity fly from her fingers. Or that she was capable of killing something. The only things she'd beaten up previously to this were punching bags and manikins. She had no idea how to be a Faerie.

What she did know, thanks to good old mom and dad, was that the tribe of Fae he'd surely been taught about was different than her tribe, but that wasn't saying a whole lot except that her tribe wasn't addicted to humans. She was a good witch, not a bad one. Her people were the ones that had kept the bad Fae under control. Or tried to, anyway.

"My parents took me away from our people when I was a little girl," she told him. "I grew up with them in China, and I was raised just like any other human kid. They didn't even tell me what I was until I was sixteen. I had no idea that I was capable of any of this…stuff…until it happened."

"Why did they take you away?"

He was being weirdly calm about all of this. If his accent hadn't given him away, she would never have known he was bothered by her admission at all. She'd expected him to freak out, maybe even try to hurt her. Werewolves and Fae did not have a good history together. As a matter of fact, his people used to hunt hers. Well, not hers, but the bad Fae.

"They were trying to protect me from our new prince."

"The same prince that sent us here?"

"I believe so, yes. I didn't know he was in this area until I called my mom to check in with her. When I told her I was in Seattle, she nearly had a stroke and ordered me to steal a car if I had to and get my ass straight to the airport." She smiled at the thought of her sweet, law-abiding mother encouraging her to commit a criminal act, but her smile fell from her face when she noticed that Brock was not sharing in her amusement. Of course, he didn't know her mom.

"What's he going to do with us?" he asked. "This prince of yours."

She shook her head. "I have no idea, Brock. I swear it. I don't know anything about him other than that my parents think he's a loon. And by his recent actions, I think they're probably right." She scooted back around the fire to kneel on the ground next to him, sitting back on her heals. Sincerity shone from her eyes as she said, "I'm so sorry you got pulled into all of this. I really am."

He gave her a sideways glare, one she couldn't quite decipher, and then returned his attention to the fire. The muscles in his jaw clenched and unclenched, and his brows were drawn together over his expressive eyes in a scowl.

Okay. Maybe he wasn't taking this as calmly as she had

thought. But still, the accent had gone away again, so it couldn't be all that bad.

She placed her hand on his arm, but pulled her hand back when his muscles jumped beneath her touch. Determined to cross the invisible chasm that was now between them thanks to her big mouth, she tried again, and this time he allowed her to touch him. "My people aren't like the ones the werewolves fought. I swear it. As a matter of fact, from what my parent's history lessons taught me, we fought the same enemy."

He looked at her then, his scowl deepening. "You fought your own people?" he asked a bit sarcastically.

"They're a different tribe of Fae. My people will never be angels, but my tribe isn't evil. The ones you fought would take out every human on the planet if they could, without remorse. Then they would turn on the creatures that were left, and then they'd go after each other. They feed off other's life forces, or souls, or chi, or whatever you want to call it. It's like the best, most addictive drug ever to them. The more they get, the more they want until they're crazed from it."

He was nodding along with her explanation. "My kind hunted your kind. Killed them all off, or so we thought."

"Not all of them. The ones that had managed to escape the slaughter were sent away." At his questioning look, she clarified, "They were locked away in another world. Another dimension."

"How? By who?"

"By the prince," she answered. "From what I understand."

"But you're saying you are not one of these creatures?"

"No," she said firmly. "I am not. My people are wood-land Fae. We gain our energy by being around this." She waved her hand at the forest around them. "We get high from the trees, and the flowers, and the animals."

He gave her a look of disbelief.

"What? We do. Just because I'm not a survivalist does not mean I'm not outdoorsy," she insisted. "We thrive from the simple things in life- good food, dancing…sex. We get our thrills from watching a storm roll in, or skinny-dipping in a hot spring," she teased, but he didn't even crack a smile, so she got serious again and continued. "Not from sucking the life from others, but from sharing their life force." She shrugged. "It sounds boring, I know."

But he shook his head. "No, sunshine. It's not boring. It's like us. Wolves are strongly connected to the mysteries of nature. How do you think we do what we do?"

His use of his nickname for her was encouraging. She scooted a bit closer to him, but he leaned away.

Okay, maybe it *was* a bit too soon. She sat back again, giving him his space, and turned her palms to the dying fire.

"What else can you do?" he asked, eyeing her up and down.

She shrugged. "Honestly, I don't know. I never needed to tap into that side of myself, until now. Actually, I've worked hard to avoid it." Thinking about it a minute, something suddenly became very clear to her. "*That's* why I've always been so good at kickboxing, I bet! Even though I can't walk three feet down the sidewalk without tripping over my own feet." It suddenly all made sense.

"I'll stoke that up again," he told her, indicating the

dying fire. "We should get some sleep." Rising to his feet, he slipped on his clean cargos and went to the other side of the spring to find some firewood.

"Sleep, he says." Heather sighed, watching him with longing, then pulled on her yoga pants and headed into the trees for a little private time.

"Don't go too far," he called out sternly.

She smiled. At least he was still concerned about her safety. That had to be a good sign.

CHAPTER 11

Brock was still awake when the sun rose the next morning. He'd been awake all night keeping the fire alive while Heather tossed restlessly in her sleep on the damp ground.

Watching her now, it was hard to believe what she'd told him last night. A Faerie? Clumsy, straightforward, sexy, city dwelling, adorable Heather was one of the Fae? He was having a difficult time wrapping his brain around it. What he'd said earlier was true though; he should've known by the way she smelled. Her scent attracted him like a bear to honey. Or rather a wolf. Just being near her woke up every nerve in his body. The way her pretty eyes were always dancing with mischief as her lush curves enchanted him with every move she made, she was a nymph of nature calling to the animal in him.

But if she was one of them, what was the point of this stupid game they were playing? Why had the prince thrown them here together after finding out that Brock wanted her? What was he hoping to achieve?

These questions and others had kept him from getting any sleep, and he still wasn't any closer to having an answer for any of them. But if there was one thing he knew from all of the old stories he'd been told, it's that the Fae never did anything without a reason. And that reason was usually one of complete fucked-up-ness.

Like so they could feed off of the souls of humans.

Brock was a relatively young wolf; he hadn't been around yet when the wars were going on hundreds of years before. But he'd heard the stories. All of those people that died in Europe in the early 1300's? Yeah, those deaths weren't all from famine and disease, although those things sure came in handy when it came to explaining away the real reasons.

According to the stories passed down by the were-wolves that had been there, nearly half of those deaths were caused from Faeries and their addiction to human energy. The symptoms of the victims were similar to that of starvation and therefore hadn't stood out as anything stranger than normal back then. The person would continue to live…zombie-like…for a week, or maybe two, as their body shut down little by little every day until finally, one day, they just didn't wake up again. Just like a seriously ill person.

No one knew what had made the previously mischievous but reclusive Fae start feeding on humans after living side by side with them for so many years. Until that had started, they'd easily lived in peace together since the humans had first evolved. Back then, the Fae were no more than a bedtime story told to human children to keep them out of trouble, or to encourage them to follow their dreams and find that pot of gold at the end of the rainbow.

When the rest of the supernatural world had figured out what was going on, the others had been hesitant to get involved with anything not having to do with their own kind. But the werewolves had volunteered to bond together to fight them. It was the one time in history that the packs had put aside their own differences and joined together for a common cause.

Because in spite of the fact that humans were afraid of, and therefor hunted, anything that was different than them (often with good reason), the wolves couldn't just stand by and watch them be exterminated. It would throw off the balance of nature, maybe never to be righted again. So, they'd become hunters of the Fae. Slowly, but surely, they'd killed them all off.

Or so they'd believed.

But if what Heather had told him was true, the Fae still lived. And more importantly, there were different tribes of them. A previously unknown fact as far as Brock knew.

He needed to get out of this place, and warn Cedric, the local pack leader here in Seattle. He would know what to do.

Brock stood and started kicking dirt over the fire as his thoughts drifted back to his one and only meeting with the Scottish alpha wolf shortly after he'd arrived in the States. As was required when visiting outside of your own lands, he'd gone to the pack leader's home on the outskirts of Seattle to ask his permission to stay in their territory for a while.

"How long is 'a while'?" Cedric had asked.

"Until I can win over the girl, at the very least." Brock grinned.

"The friend?"

"Yes. Heather Knight is her name."

The alpha leaned back in his chair and crossed his arms over his massive chest. "Ye 'ave my permission tae stay. On one condition."

Brock's "thank you" stuck in his throat. "What condition is that?"

Leaning forward in his chair, Cedric speared him with those eerie white eyes of his. "Ye see, I ken that yer no' telling me the entire truth. There's more tae yer story, wee pup. But I'm willin' tae let ye get more comfortable here 'n' with me. I ken it's hard to trust when ye 'ave been on yer own for a while."

"Aye, I ken that yer without pack," Cedric answered his look of surprise. "And until I ken more aboot ye, I'm no' inclined to bring ye into mine. Ye ken?"

"Sure. I understand. And thank you, for letting me stay."

"Och. Aye. Now git yer arse out of here before the other lads show up and give ye a hard time. They will nae harm ye. Ye 'ave my word."

The two wolves stood and shook hands.

"Thank you, again. I really appreciate it," Brock told him at the door.

"Take this just in case I need ye." He handed Brock a cell

phone. "Now, go get yer lass." Cedric grinned as he closed the door in his face.

EVEN IN JUST THAT short time he'd been around him, he'd liked Cedric right from the start. Unlike his previous alpha, Cedric carried his role of pack leader with a mature, confident strength, not cockiness. Maybe, if things worked out, he'd talk to him about staying in the area a little longer.

An ache filled his chest as he thought of being around a pack again. Even one he wasn't a member of. It wasn't natural for him to be off on his own like he'd been. Of course, that was the whole point of being banned. Most wolves evicted from their pack didn't survive the beat down that accompanied it, and they preferred it that way. Dying was a better option than living such a lonely existence. It was purely bad luck that he had lived through it.

His thoughts drifted to Lucian: His oldest friend, and the reason he found himself in this situation if you got right down to it. He really hoped the bastard appreciated what he'd done for him, although somehow he doubted it. Lucian had always been too self-absorbed, to the extent that Brock had often wondered if his lifelong friend truly cared about anyone but himself.

If he had the choice to do it all over again, to choose between saving himself or his friend, he didn't know that he would make the same choice.

Brock shook off the thoughts of his past as his gaze wandered back to the lovely female snoring next to the smoldering ashes of the fire. Her snores were soft and ladylike, just like her, and he smiled in spite of his trepidations. He'd gotten the girl. But he'd lost the phone Cedric had given him. Not a good way to gain the trust of the Kincaid pack if the alpha was, in fact, trying to reach him. But there wasn't much he could do about it at the moment.

There was, however, something he could do about the girl. If she was Fae as she claimed, this relationship wouldn't last once they got back to the real world. It couldn't. Werewolves and Fae were sworn enemies, and had been for hundreds of years. Even if he accepted her as his mate, other wolves wouldn't. And the Fae wouldn't accept him either. He would forever be protecting his mate from being attacked and quite possibly killed by others of their own kind. She'd be an outcast. Like him. And he cared about her too much already to do that to her.

He needed to end this thing between them. Now.

As if she could feel his attention on her, her eyes fluttered open, blinking in the light of morning. When she saw him standing there, she smiled up at him and her entire face lit up like a ray of much needed sunshine. He felt like an ass when that smile faltered because he didn't reciprocate, but he'd never been very good at hiding his feelings.

She got stiffly to her feet and brushed off her clothes. "What's wrong?" she asked. "What's happened?"

He knew he looked like he'd just lost his favorite snuggly. But he couldn't help it. He would miss her. He opened his mouth to tell her what he'd been thinking, to let her know that the night before had truly meant more to him than she would ever know, but that they needed to go their separate ways once they got out of here. But all that came out was, "Nothing. We just need to go, so we can get the fuck out of here."

She eyed him up and down, but only said, "Okay. Just give me a few minutes."

He watched her walk into the shelter of the trees as his heart fractured within his chest, then he finished putting out the fire and laced up his boots. He released a frustrated breath.

Dammit.

Brock was used to being alone. He'd been alone for a few years now. No pack. No friends. His parents had died when he was very young. So why did the thought of never seeing this one particular female again bother him so much? A female he'd only known for a few days?

He sighed heavily. Realistically, he'd only known her for a few days, but his soul felt like he'd been searching for her for a long, long, time.

Well, he'd just have to get over it. There were other females in the world. Lots of them. Human females. Shifter females. He could have any one of them he wanted.

Except he didn't want any of those nameless, faceless women. He wanted Heather.

He kicked at a few last burning embers in frustration, then kicked at them harder when they refused to go out. With a curse he knelt down on one knee to use his hands, and then he realized why those embers were still burning.

Because it wasn't embers he saw in the dirt. It was a

half buried golden coin, glinting up at him like there was not a cloud in the sky.

"Are you fucking kidding me?" he muttered. A trickle of nervous sweat meandered down his temple, and he wiped it away impatiently. Brock looked around for Heather, but she was nowhere in sight. "Heather!" He waited for her to respond or come wandering out of the fog, and even debated going in after her after a few minutes had gone by with no sign of her. Then he felt something hit the toe of his boot.

The coin had moved all on its own and was now lying right next to his foot.

"Ah, fuck it."

Closing his eyes and saying a quick prayer to anyone who happened to be listening, he picked it up and threw it in the air. "Heads!" he called loud and clear. Catching it and flipping it over onto his opposite hand, he sent up another quick prayer for good measure and took a deep breath before he forced himself to look.

The prince's face looked back at him.

"Whoo!" he whooped to the sky, and stuck it in his pocket with the other one. Take that, you bastard. Maybe they'd get a change of clothes or something. Or a toothbrush. He smiled, thinking how happy Heather was gonna be when he told her what had happened while she was gone. He waited for a bit, but nothing dropped out of the sky. Nothing appeared out of the mist.

Maybe that was what he got for winning. A whole lot of nothing happening. And that was just fine with him.

Kneeling at the edge of the spring, he stuck his hands into the water to splash some of it on his face. With a yell, he yanked them back out again and looked at the blisters rising on his hands in disbelief. The water that had been pleasantly heated while they'd bathed the night before was now scalding hot.

"What the fuck?" he exclaimed.

They were burned from the scalding hot water. The shit was practically boiling.

A gurgling sound pulled his attention from his burned hands back to the water. As he watched, a bubble floated to the surface of the spring, then another, and another. More and more of them until the water was heated to a roiling boil. Steam rose in a thick curtain from the surface as the hot water dissipated in the cool morning air.

"Well, hell." It was a good thing they hadn't jumped in for a morning bath. They would've ended up more like flavoring for the soup.

Brock stood up and backed away, noticing something weird with the water level. It was rising. Rapidly. He squinted into the thickening fog and searched the trees again. "Heather!" he shouted. "Heather!!"

The water started to trickle over the rocky sides, and Brock danced back out of its way. Once it hit the grass, some of it soaked into the ground, but not enough. The ground was already over saturated, and it quickly began to flood the area. He needed to get to the other side of the spring to the thicker set of trees where Heather had disappeared before he got cut off from her.

No sooner had the thought entered his mind than the spring erupted, spewing a fifty-foot stream of boiling water into the air. Heart pounding, he took off running before it could fall back down to land on him, skirting the edge of the overflowing water. Drops of hot water rained on him from the fountain, burning him, but he ignored them. Keeping his eye on the water he pumped his arms and legs harder. He was almost around it.

The ground rumbled beneath him and Brock stumbled as another burst of water shot into the air not ten feet from him, and twice as high this time. Waves of it came rolling rapidly toward him.

He wasn't going to make it.

CHAPTER 12

Heather yanked up her yoga pants and prayed that the leaves she'd just used weren't of the poison oak variety. That would so completely suck. She winced slightly as she adjusted her clothing. She was sore, but in the most wonderful way. After all, Brock was a large guy. All over.

Nothing a good soak in the hot spring won't cure.

A small smile curved her mouth as she thought of what Brock's reaction was going to be when she returned only to strip down right in front of him. She couldn't blame him for what was bothering him this morning, but if last night was any indication, the sight of her bare behind should be enough to pull him out of his funk.

Funny. She'd never been shy about sex, as long as the lights were dimmed. Or better yet, off completely so her partner couldn't see her. Once she could get a guy into bed, her naturally passionate nature took over, making up for her less than perfect body. Keeping a guy in her bed?

That was a different story. She'd yet to find one that wanted repeat action, even though every single one of them had all but bowed and kissed her feet after a night with her. She knew it was because she was a plus-size girl. No guy wanted to be seen with anything less than a Barbie doll these days. It would ruin their rep or whatever.

Personally, she thought it was because their balls were quite small. Too small to stand up to society. Or maybe it was the lack of better prospects at the time that steered them to her bed, and nothing else.

But for the first time in her life, she didn't feel any trepidation at all about prancing around completely naked in front of a guy. But Brock wasn't just any guy, and he honestly seemed to have a true appreciation for her figure, chubby rolls and all.

Unless it was only because she happened to be the only female here, and like most of the guys she came across (usually around last call at whatever bar she happened to be in, if she were to be honest with herself), he wasn't one to turn down an opportunity.

Or maybe he really just likes you. Why else would his eyes light up the way they do whenever he looks at you? Heather berated herself for her negative thoughts as soon as she thought them. She was normally a pretty positive kind of person. But sometimes, it was really hard to stay positive about something that the rest of the world insisted you should feel ashamed of. After a while, you can't help but start to believe them.

A few feet away, she spotted a clump of viney-looking things that didn't look too rough or too sappy. Breaking off one of the branches, she sniffed it, then touched the tip of her tongue to it. Just a branch. Perfect. She used the broken greenery to scrub at her teeth.

See? She could adapt.

While she brushed, she kept a keen eye out for anything strange, but all was peaceful, and her thoughts wandered back to her anticipation of what she hoped would be a repeat of the night before. Was it so hard to believe that maybe, just maybe, he was actually attracted to girls that had a little more meat on them? Maybe he was. Even though she wasn't exactly bikini model material, she wasn't completely repulsive.

Running her tongue over her teeth, she searched for any spots she'd missed and then tossed the branch aside. Different colors to her left caught her eye and she wandered over to a small bush growing near the base of one of the never-ending pine trees. Bending down, she carefully moved the thorny branches aside to reveal a handful of dark purple berries.

Could it be? Plucking one from its home, she took a small bite. It was! Wild blackberries! Thrilled to have something to eat, however meager, that wasn't a mutant-cat-thing, she eagerly filled her shirt with every ripe berry on the bush. It wasn't much, but it was enough to share.

"Heather!"

Her head whipped around at the distant sound of Brock's voice. That didn't sound good.

"Heather!!"

Why did he sound so far away? She hadn't been out here for that long, had she? She couldn't have wandered away that far.

"I'm coming!" she yelled through the fog.

She'd just started heading back toward the spring when the ground shook violently beneath her feet. Dropping the berries, she lurched toward Brock's voice, moving as fast as she dared as the ground rippled beneath her feet. She swerved to miss a tree trunk but a branch snaked out in front of her and she tripped, landing hard face down in the dirt and pine needles. Pushing herself to her feet, she struggled on until she came to the break in the never-ending trees and the spring was in sight.

Only it wasn't a spring anymore. It was a freakin' geyser.

Her mouth dropped open as she stared up at the steaming tower of water spewing from the earth.

"Get back!!" Brock bellowed at her.

He was running full out toward her, sort of. Another spout of water was bursting through the ground, blocking his way. The small clearing was flooding rapidly, and she could see he was trying to get around the advancing water before it cut her off from him completely. The ground rumbled again and the geysers shot up even higher. With a roar, Brock splashed through the water at full speed.

He grabbed her hand as he ran past her and pulled her along with him. "Come on! We 'ave tae go. Now!"

She turned to run and stumbled over a rock in true Heather fashion, and he wrapped an arm around her waist, hauling her along with him until they'd gotten far enough away. When they were out of range of the quaking ground, he slowed to a jog, setting her on her feet and making sure she had her balance before letting go of her waist.

"What the hell was that?" she panted.

"I won a coin toss."

She stared at him in disbelief, but he grabbed her hand and tugged her along behind him before she could say anything else. If this was what happened when he won, she'd hate to see what would've gone down if he'd lost.

He kept them at a pace that she could barely keep up with, but didn't slow down for her this time. Every few seconds, he'd look back over his shoulder, and urge her to keep going.

They must have run for at least a mile before Heather finally staggered to a stop. Leaning over, she put her hands on her knees and tried to breath. She hated how exhausted she was, but marathon running had never been her thing.

"We should keep going." Brock had circled back to her and now stood hovering at her side. The son of a bitch wasn't even out of breath.

She held up one hand. "I…just…need…a few… seconds," she panted. "To catch my breath."

He looked back toward where they'd come from with an anxious expression, but finally, he gave a curt nod. "Okay."

It took her more like a minute, but eventually she started breathing somewhat normally again. "All right," she said as she straightened up. "I'm good."

"We can probably just…"

Brock didn't finish what he'd been about to say. Heather opened her mouth to ask what was wrong when she heard it too. The roar of rushing water. It was getting louder now with every second, and it was coming straight toward them.

"Go! Go!" Brock shouted, urging her forward with a hand on the small of her back.

Heather willed her tired limbs to move and took off running again in no particular direction except away from the tidal wave coming at them. They ran blindly through the fog, dodging trees and briars.

"Look for high ground!" Brock shouted.

Out of the corner of her eye, Heather caught a glimpse of something running with them, low to the ground. She looked harder. It was one of those cat things. As she watched, it made a sharp turn and took off through the fog.

"This way!" Grabbing his hand, she pulled him to the right, following it. It was more familiar with this place then they were, and animals usually had a sense for getting out of danger.

The roar of the water was deafening now, the air so hot and humid her clothes were sticking to her and she could barely breathe. It felt like she was in a kettle of boiling water, seasoned with pine needles. Heather could no longer hear Brock running behind her, but didn't need to risk looking back to check on him. She could feel him behind her, silently urging her on.

She was running so hard, she couldn't have stopped if she wanted to when the stream they'd been following the day before suddenly appeared in front of her. She barreled through the icy water, emerging on the other side and running up the bank to higher ground.

At the top, she stopped and turned and Brock did the same. She concentrated on not throwing up while they watched the wave of floodwater coming at them. As the edge of it hit the stream, it seemed to lose some of its momentum.

"I think we're okay here," Brock voiced the same thing she'd been thinking. Studying the landscape as far as he could see, he nodded. "I think we're high enough."

Keeping a close eye on the rapidly swelling stream, she stated the obvious. "Glad it waited for us to get out before it decided to turn into a water spout."

"It wasn't just a water spout, we would've been soup if we'd still been in there," Brock told her.

"Soup?"

"The water started to boil while you were gone."

"Boil?" She knew she was repeating everything he'd just said like an idiot, but she couldn't seem to stop herself.

He held out his bright red hands for her to see. "I scalded my hands when I stuck them in the water to wash my face. They were blistered when I first pulled them out. If I'd waited a few more seconds, it would've cooked the muscle right off my bones." Dropping his hands, he pointed with his chin. "Here it comes."

They held their breath as the highest part of the wave made its way toward them, destroying everything in its wake like a steamroller. It took down thirty-foot trees effortlessly, tossing them about like toothpicks in the muddy waters and cutting a path as far as the eye could see. As it hit the stream, it seemed to pause, weighing its options. The water hissed loudly as the two temperatures mixed, then with a renewed surge of strength, it plowed through the cold water and headed their way.

"It's like it's alive or something," she breathed in awe.

Brock took her by the wrist and began to back up. "We're nae high enough."

Heather squinted through the cloud of steam created by the stream, like cold water hitting a hot frying pan. Rather than slowing it down, the wave seemed to be gaining power as it plowed up the bank toward the hill they were on. Chunks of the ground gave way as the water pounded toward them, creating a mudslide above it. It edged ever closer to them until the ground began to slip from under her feet as she tried to back away.

"Heather! Grab my hand!" Brock shouted.

She reached back for him but before he could get a good grip, the water surged up and slammed into her, sucking her down and tossing her head over heels until she didn't know which way was up. At least the cold stream had cooled the water down enough so she wasn't being boiled alive. However, she now had other things to worry about.

Her lungs were screaming for air when she slammed into a tree trunk floating downstream. She wrapped her arms around it, letting it carry her along. Her face broke the surface of the water and she sucked in a quick breath before she was pushed under again. The rough bark tore through her clothes to the soft skin beneath, leaving stinging scrapes covering her chest and arms, but she hung on to that tree with everything in her.

The second time she came up, she heard Brock screaming her name from far away, but when she opened her mouth to answer him water poured in as she went under again. Rolling over and over with the log, she finally broke the surface again just when she thought she was surely going to drown. Sputtering and coughing, she stayed above water this time as she floated along with the floodwaters.

Drawing her first deep breath since she'd gone under, she croaked out, "Brock!" She pulled herself up higher on the log and searched the water around her. "Brock!" she screamed, louder this time.

But he wasn't there. She was gearing up to yell for him again when she noticed the river she was floating in was picking up speed, and fast. And the roar of the water was getting louder. As her log floaty spun around in the current, she saw the top of a pine disappear into thin air in front of her, followed by the sound of a large explosion. Splinters flew back up into the air. All that was left of the majestic tree.

Heather closed her eyes, praying to any gods who were listening that it wasn't what it appeared. But apparently there were no gods around at the moment, for when she opened them again, the log was wrenched from her arms as they were both swept over the edge of the waterfall.

CHAPTER 13

Brock fought the current and leaped to the side, all four paws scurrying for purchase on the muddy ground as he tried to avoid being sucked back into the floodwaters.

He'd watched with his heart in his throat as Heather had disappeared over the edge of the waterfall. Her terrified scream had triggered a corresponding reaction in him, bringing on the change without warning. He'd screamed with her as his body had contorted, throwing him mid-change right into the water with her.

Swept along with the raging water, he knew better than to try and fight it, instead he just took a breath whenever he could and tried to avoid colliding with large debris. As soon as he'd regained some control in the swirling water, he'd managed to paddle over to the side and drag himself up onto the muddy bank.

He looked out over the devastation the water had left behind. The little stream they'd been following, their only landmark in this crazy place, appeared to have been transformed into something that resembled more of a river about the size of the Amazon. Of course that was only speculation. With the ever-present fog obscuring his view, he could only hazard a guess as to how large it had grown.

All of the trees anywhere near it were gone, washed away in the power of the flood. Which meant so were the pieces of clothing he'd tied to them to mark his way back to where he'd landed. Hell, the entire area he'd previously travelled was probably under water.

Sprinting along with the rushing river, he slid to a stop at the edge of the waterfall, searching below for any sign of Heather. He didn't see anything floating in the water or washed up onto the bank. Not a scrap of clothing, nothing. Throwing his head back, he howled his anguish to the sky.

Pacing back and forth, he searched the edge for an accessible way down. However, all he saw was the sheer side of a rocky cliff. There was nothing to dig his claws into, nothing to break his slide. And at the bottom were more of the never-ending, fucking pine trees. He had to be at least a few hundred feet up. The towering trees resembled tiny plastic pieces of a child's toy rather than the majestic evergreens that they were. If he tried to slide down the rock he'd end up impaled on the pointy tip of one of those trees.

He watched the churning water as another uprooted tree was swept over the edge to shatter at the bottom like it was nothing but a matchstick. Could Faeries die from a fall like that?

The thought left him reeling. He had to get down

there, and fast. Running horizontal to the edge of the cliff, he finally found a traversable gradient about a half-mile away and bounded over the side. Half running and half skidding down the rock, he made his way to the bottom in record time.

Backtracking to the water, he put his nose to the ground and searched for signs of his female. Watching her fall off the edge of the earth had brought a simple clarity to what was between them. He couldn't lose her now. Not now. Not when he'd just realized how much he needed her. And fuck the fact that she was Fae and he was a shifter. He didn't belong to a pack. He had no one to protest his choice of a mate. They'd move around a lot. Stay under the radar. He'd protect her.

He didn't want to be alone anymore.

Fortified with a new determination, he followed the edge of the water. A few miles downstream, he caught a trace of her scent. Twenty feet inland, he found her. It looked like she had dragged herself by the elbows as far as she could away from the edge of the water before collapsing in the soft pine needles under a massive pine tree.

She was unconscious, black and blue and bloody from numerous cuts and scrapes, but she was alive. He could hear her heart beating. It was strong and steady. Her left arm and right calf were twisted at weird angles, the bones broken in numerous locations.

He nudged her limp body with his nose, then stepped over her to try again on her other side. She didn't respond.

Whining with worry and fear, he shook the water from his fur and paced back and forth a few times before he sat down next to her. He tried to calm himself enough to change back so he could help her. It took him a good while and some chanting of mantras, but he finally did it.

Back in human form, he rolled her onto her back and pulled her limp body halfway onto his lap. "Come on, sunshine. Wake up for me." Peeling her wet hair from her face, he watched her eyelids flutter briefly. "That's it. Come on. Wake up for me now." He put his palm against her cheek, one of the few places he could see that wasn't bruised or bleeding, and kissed her on the forehead. "Heather. Please. I need you tae wake up and let me know that I can stop freaking out. Come on, sunshine."

He shook her gently and she moaned in protest, her lids fluttering again.

"That's it. Wake up and ye can yell at me all ye want for causin' ye discomfort. But until then, I'm going tae keep bugging ye." He shook her again.

"Ow," she croaked.

It was the most beautiful sound he'd ever heard. He grinned like an idiot and pulled her against his chest, hugging her close in spite of her weak protests.

Then she passed out again.

He let her be this time, as hard as it was for him to see her in such a state. It would be easier for her when he set her broken limbs. Gritting his teeth, he laid her back down and did what needed to be done quickly and effi-ciently, ripping her thin, running jacket in half to bind her newly set bones as best he could.

For a long time afterward, he sat naked in the mud with her on his lap, just watching her breathe. As her chest rose and fell in a steady cadence, his thoughts drifted back to the epiphany he'd had when she'd gone over the waterfall. He'd meant every word. Heather was his now, and he was hers. She wasn't your usual Faerie, and he was a wolf without a pack. Somehow, they'd carve their way in this world. Together. And if her prince didn't like it, he could shove it where the sun didn't shine.

Something teased the edge of his memory when he thought of the Fae prince. Something important. But no matter how hard he racked his brain, it remained just out of his reach.

He sighed, too distraught to worry about it now, and worried instead about what Heather would say when she found out the truth about him.

THREE YEARS Earlier

BROCK STOOD in a submissive pose in front of his alpha, waiting for him to declare his decision. Sweat trickled down his spine, not entirely caused by the unusually warm sun beating down upon the back of his neck. Behind him, the rest of the werewolf pack moved about restlessly, some already in the process of changing in anticipation of the bloodletting that was surely about to happen.

He glanced over to his right toward his lifelong friend, trying to read how he was feeling about all of this in his stormy grey eyes. That face was as familiar to him as his own, but his only friend refused to look at him, keeping his eyes somewhere in the vicinity behind his left shoulder. Was it from guilt, or was he really that selfish?

Brock sighed inwardly. He didn't know why he was surprised. And he supposed his friend appearing indifferent was for the better. No one would guess the truth of what had really happened to bring them both to this point in time.

"Brock Hume, please come forward tae me." Thomas, the alpha male of this unruly Scottish pack, spoke quietly but firmly. Brock took a few steps forward, keeping his head bowed and his eyes lowered. The thick-soled boots of his alpha entered his line of vision, and beside him, the silver-tipped boots of his new advisor who was even now whispering in the pack leader's ear.

Low growls of approval vibrated the air around him as the pack surged forward with him, eager to get on with the ritual they were certain was about to happen. Bones cracked and fluid gushed as more of them gave in to the change, bloodlust overtaking them until they were helpless against it.

Thomas bared his teeth at the wolves, calling for order. Once they'd quieted down to a low roar, he turned his attention to the young werewolf awaiting his decision. Brock held his breath, even though he knew what was coming. There was no other choice to be made, really. Not with him having just spoken his confession loud and clear in front of the entire pack and the evidence of Sara's growing belly: The belly that was growing in spite of the fact that her husband had been off working with another pack for the past eight months with no time for a conjugal visit.

Thomas' voice rang across the clearing, the Scottish brogue rolling from his tongue that Brock had since worked hard to lose. "Brock Hume! Ya have, by yer own admission, broken one o' our most sacred laws."

A few high-pitched howls rose into the air behind him.

"Th' punishment for this crime, as stated in our pack law, tis non-negotiable." He paused until Brock looked up at him. Although his features were set in stone, the remorse he was feeling shone behind his eyes. But as the alpha of the pack, Thomas had no choice but to condemn him to his punishment. Brock knew this, and did not hold it against this male that had taken him in and helped raise him to be the male that he was.

Thomas' voice broke as he threw down the gauntlet. "As o' this moment, ye are nae longer a member of this pack." He had to shout now to be heard above the snarls and howling that broke out around them, his hands fisted at his sides and his face twisting as he fought his own change that was trying to overtake him. "Brock Hume, if ya live through this, ye are exiled from our lands, never tae return or contact us again. Ye are a siubhal, a lone wolf, from this day forward."

This last was spoken in more of a deep growl than anything else as the alpha dropped to the ground, the change fully over-taking him. A flash of fear shot through Brock, even though he'd known this was coming, as the sounds of breaking bones and tearing flesh echoed around him.

He ground his jaw together and willed his own change to take him before the first attack came from his former pack mates. As he dropped to the ground, he glared at Thomas' advisor, the only one there still in his human form.

He was smiling.

EVENTUALLY, Brock realized that his entire body was covered in gooseflesh and he was shivering. Whether from the cold or the awful memories, he couldn't say. Gathering Heather into his arms, he got to his feet, easily lifting her with him. He wanted to get as far away as possible from this damn water before night came.

Heading into the misty forest, he pondered more deeply the implications of his decision to keep this woman. He realized that he was going to have to tell her why he was without a pack. He wanted no more secrets between them. He just hoped that she would understand and that he could convince her to stay with him. There were a lot of reasons why she would think they shouldn't be together.

His jaw set in a stubborn line. She would stay with him, and he would make her happy. As soon as they got the fuck out of this place.

Once he'd gotten far enough away for his own comfort, he found some shelter under a thick cluster of trees that were up on a slight rise. Now that the tidal wave had leveled out, if worse came to worse and the water made its way toward them, he'd have time to get them to safety.

Setting her down carefully so as not to jar her healing bones before they'd had a chance to set properly, he set about making a fire to keep them warm. Moving her closer to the heat, he cuddled up behind her to share her heat and watch the flames. His stomach growled to protest the loss of their skoochat that day, but it was just going to have to wait. There was no way in hell he was leaving her here alone and injured and unable to defend herself.

As night fell, he fed the flames and tried to keep her warm. He worried about her clothes still being wet, but if he took them off, she'd be as bare as he was to the chilly night air. And they were beginning to dry already, so he left them on for now. After the heat of the boiling flood, it seemed unusually cold.

He reached over his head to the small pile of wood he'd gathered there and threw another small log onto the fire, watching the sparks dance above the flames. Heather moaned in her sleep, drawing his eyes back to her flawless profile. Freckles stood out starkly against her pale skin, and he pulled some leaves out of her damp hair.

The muscles in his jaw clenched as he watched her try to get into a more comfortable position, and then moan in pain without waking. He helped her roll over carefully, pulling her up close to him again.

He was so done with this place. It was time to get them the fuck out of there, come hell…he snorted quietly…or high water. Tomorrow he would find the place he'd started. He'd carry her the entire way if need be, and get them home.

He needed to make plans, needed to figure out how they were going to get around the bias they would receive for being together. But his lack of sleep the night before and the excitement of the day caught up to him, and he finally gave up and closed his eyes.

WHEN HE WOKE up a few hours later, there was a pile of dry clothes for him to wear folded by the fire. He wanted to throw them into the flames and scream his frustration, but he did neither. Checking on Heather, he found her clothes and hair were almost completely dry, and she seemed to be sleeping more peacefully.

He kicked dirt over the smoldering fire and donned his new clothes with silent determination, then he lifted Heather up into a sitting position. Brushing her off as well as he could, he settled her in his arms and started walking back toward the water, hoping he'd find some remnant of the trail he'd left.

It wasn't anywhere near morning yet, but he could see through the darkness as well as he could see through the fog. Maybe he should leave new markers, so he wasn't walking around in circles. Gathering Heather's unconscious form into one arm, he extended his claws and used his free hand to slash at the tree trunks as he passed. Possibly with a little more force than was really necessary.

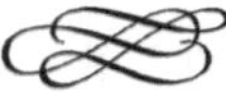

Cedric Kincaid, six feet seven inches of pure alpha and head of the Seattle area werewolf pack, cocked his dark head to the side and dug his fingers into the flesh of Lucian's throat. He was getting damned sick and tired of this young pup and his bad attitude.

"Haud yer wheesht!" he growled. "I won't listen tae any more of yer nonsense. Do ye ken?" He could feel the restless tension in the air coming from the other wolves in the pack, but he felt no fear, even with his back to them. They were riled up due to what was going on, but they were loyal to him. On that he would bet his life. They'd been together living as a pack and a family for a long time.

This young one in his grip? Not so much. He still needed to learn his place.

Lucian glared at him with grey eyes that reminded him of a stormy sea. After a tense moment, he lowered his lids and turned his face away as much as he could with

Cedric's large hand cutting off his airway, exposing his throat in a sign of submission.

Cedric pulled his lips back in a snarl, exposing his elongated canines, and clamped them down around the life-giving artery in Lucian's throat. He pressed down just enough to break the skin, and growled low in his throat until he felt the fight leave the pup's body as he submitted fully to his alpha.

Releasing his teeth and his hand at the same time, he dropped Lucian to the floor at his feet and waited for him to get up before he spoke. "If ye 'ave an issue with what I'm suggesting, we will discuss it. But I'm no' going to put up with yer outbursts."

"I meant nae disrespect," Lucian gritted out.

Cedric narrowed his eyes at his tone but said nothing more. The boy had pride, and something else, some lingering frustration that stemmed from something that had happened before they'd found him. He'd always been a wee bit cocky, but lately his pent up anger had been brewing so hot inside that Cedric was afraid the top was going to blow off the pot. He just hoped that anger didn't boil over to burn them all during a life and death situation.

Turning to the other two wolves in his small pack, he observed their distinctive reactions to Lucian's behavior.

Duncan's green eyes danced with merriment, as usual. He seemed to find the entire situation amusing. It took a hell of a lot more than a spat between pack mates to worry him. His mouth twisted up in a crooked smile as he shook his head at Lucian. "When are ye aft tae learn, wee pup?"

Lucian's jaw flexed as he speared Duncan with his stormy gaze, but the older wolf only slapped him on the back with a show of good-natured commiserating. "Come on. Let's hear th' rest o' what Cedric has tae say before ya go off all half cocked." Throwing an arm over Lucian's stiff shoulders, he led him past Marc and into the living room of Cedric's apartment. Plunking down onto the couch, he pulled Lucian down beside him.

Marc watched them with his fathomless dark eyes, almost as dark as his hair, then chose the chair farthest from them and sat down. Keeping a close eye on Lucian's auburn head, he waited for Cedric to continue their conversation.

As they got settled, Cedric reached up and pulled the tie from his long, black, wavy hair. Smoothing the flyaways back from his face with his hands, he gathered the mass together at the nape of his neck and tied it back again. Then he lifted his ice-blue eyes and looked at each member of his pack in turn as he spoke, taking in their reactions.

"So, as I was saying afore I was sae rudely interrupted, I had a brief visit with th' wolf that helped our friend's female escape China: Brock Hume."

Lucian's only reaction to the other male's name this time was a slight ticking in the muscle of his jaw.

Cedric hesitated a moment to see if there was another outburst coming, but Lucian kept his palms flat on his thighs and his eyes on the floor at his feet. Of course, Duncan's firm grip on his shoulder may have had something to do with that. "Whit dae ye ken about the lad, Lucian?" he asked.

"I ken nothing about him," he muttered.

"That's nae true. If it were true, ye would nae have reacted th' way ye did just a few seconds ago."

Lucian clamped his jaw together and refused to say anything more.

"Why are ye asking?" Marc wanted to know. "He's just visiting here, is he no'?"

"Aye," Cedric told him. "And I'll be th' first tae admit I dinna know anythin' else aboot the lad, except that he is withou' a pack. I was thinkin' maybe we could invite him in tae ours." He held up his hand to stop the protests before they could be voiced. "We could use another braw lad like him. Even if he does 'ave bonnie locks better than mine." He lifted a hand to his long ponytail and smiled. "He would 'ave tae earn his place first, o' course, just like ye all did." He shrugged. "I just 'ave a feeling about the pup."

Duncan was nodding his head in agreement. "I say 'aye'. Let's bring him in. Get tae know him. If ye think that he would be a good fit for us, I trust yer instincts."

Cedric turned to Marc. "Whit aboot ye? Dae ya think we should give him a chance?"

Marc's intelligent dark eyes shifted from Lucian to his alpha. "I have nae met him, but I trust ye. If yer impression of this male was that he deserves th' chance, than I say 'aye' also. However, I would like th' chance to get to know him before ya make th' offer."

Cedric nodded. "Lucian? If ye 'ave any knowledge or doubts aboot this male, now would be th' time tae tell us."

They all turned to see what he would say, but he just

shook his dark auburn head sharply to the side. "I 'ave nothin' tae say aboot him. Do as ye like."

He was hiding something. Cedric was sure of it. But if didn't want to tell him what it was, then he would proceed with his plan. "Well, all right then. As soon as I see him again, I will make th' offer for him tae stay for a while. And we'll take it from there. But remember, lads," He waited until he was sure he had all of their attention. "This is no' just my pack. It is *our* pack. I will nae invite anyone in if any one of you has an issue wit' it. A *legitimate* issue," he emphasized, crossing his arms over his muscular chest and looking back and forth between Marc and Lucian.

Marc gave him a nod while Lucian grabbed Duncan's hand and threw his arm off with a sound of disgust, much to Duncan's delight.

CHAPTER 15

Brock strode up to what used to be a harmless, trickling stream. He stopped and shifted Heather to a more comfortable position in his arms. They were on the opposite bank than they needed to be, but it was still dark, the fog heavier than normal. Without being able to see the other side, he was hesitant to try to cross it even though the current seemed quite a bit calmer here.

He was trying to decide whether to go for it and just try to get across now with an unconscious female in his arms, or to follow it upstream and watch for a less dangerous section when something bounced off of his head to land on her stomach.

"Ah! What the…?"

The words died instantly in his throat. A golden coin lay amongst the folds of her tee shirt, mocking him. Rage flooded through him and he had to take a moment to control his anger. Taking deep breaths, he counted to ten, then to twenty, before he felt the slightest bit in control again. He knew there was no avoiding it. He was going to have to toss the fucking coin.

Gently setting Heather on the ground, he took the coin from her shirt and flipped it into the air. No sense in delaying the inevitable. "Tails," he gritted through his teeth. Catching it in mid-air, he slammed it onto the back of his other hand.

The prince's smiling face grinned up at him. He looked particularly happy this time that Brock had lost.

A bubble of laughter rose up in Brock's throat. He tried to quench it, but before he knew it, he was laughing outright. Belly shaking, head thrown back, loud howls of laughter.

The fucking son of a bitch.

Gradually, his laughter turned to chuckles and the chuckles to nothing more than an occasional grunt. He wondered with no emotion whatsoever what the puppet master had in store for him this time.

Heather moaned in her sleep and he bent down to lift her back into his arms. She settled down again as soon as she felt his warmth around her. He debated whether he should find a place to hide her or keep her with him, preferably right there in his arms. Without knowing what was coming for him it was hard to know which would be safest for her. In the end, he decided to keep her with him. At least that way he knew where she was and he could protect her better.

A few more minutes passed by and nothing had jumped out of the fog at him, so he decided to just start following the river again. The sound of the flowing water was calming, in spite of his wracked nerves. Whatever was going to happen would happen, and there was nothing he could do about it. So instead of standing around waiting for it, he would keep on walking, getting them that much closer to the end of this god-forsaken game.

He'd been walking for about thirty minutes. The shot of adrenaline that had hit him when he saw the coin had worn off and now he was just…numb. Waiting. Placing one foot in front of the other on autopilot, following the river upstream.

Maybe this is the game, he thought. *Maybe this is the best game of all for him. Driving me slowly insane waiting for something to happen when nothing is going to happen.*

He started laughing again.

Heather's arm slipped to hang limply at her side and he stopped. Glancing around, he found a fallen log and headed over to it so he could sit down for a moment. He needed a break. Not from carrying her, no. She was like next to nothing in his powerful arms. He just needed a break from the waiting.

He settled her on his lap and lifted her arm and tucked it across her chest, careful of her other arm and her injury. Pushing her hair off of her shoulder, he adjusted her makeshift sling, securing the knot. "Now you can tell all your friends that I swept you off your feet and carried you away. Well, technically, the floodwaters swept you off your feet. But I picked you back up again." He pressed a light kiss to her forehead. "I'll always pick you back up again, sunshine." Her eyelids fluttered but she didn't awaken.

Taking a deep breath, he stood, not wanting to linger for too long in any one spot. He'd just taken his first step when an icy shaft of air *caressed* the side of his face, like the soft touch of a lover. His hackles rose immediately and a low growl reverberated deep in his throat. He waited, but nothing else happened. Thinking it must've been only his imagination, he lifted his foot to set off again and almost fell on top of Heather when he was physically pushed by someone behind him.

Whipping around, he bared his teeth and prepared to fight whoever or whatever was there, but there was nothing but pine trees and mist. A cold chill swept over him.

"Please tell me there are no ghosts here," he pleaded. "No ghosts. I do not DO ghosts. I'll fight any monster you can think up with a fucking smile on my face, but I can't… I can't do ghosts."

"And where the hell is the fucking sun?!" he shouted to the sky. It was still dark, and appeared to be getting darker out rather than lighter, as it should definitely be by now. Another set of icy fingers ghosted down his bare arm; startling him so much he almost dropped his precious cargo.

This time it just pissed him off. "Fine. You want to touch me? Push me? Try to freak me out? Go ahead. You won't stop me." Tucking Heather up close to him, he marched with a determined stride back to the river and continued to follow it. He kept his eyes on the ground in front of him, only glancing up once in a while to search for a section of the river that would be easy to cross.

He'd gone about three hundred feet when he saw some gentle rapids. Rapids meant rocks. And rocks meant the water wasn't as deep there. And that meant he'd be able to get across.

A smile broke out across his face and he sped up his pace. Other than a ghostly caress here and there, the spooks seemed to be pretty harmless, if unnerving and completely unconcerned about what was appropriate and what wasn't.

He'd gotten less than a few steps away from the crossing when suddenly, without warning, he was *whooshed* all the way back to the fallen log.

Grinding his jaw, he set out again, faster this time. But again, as soon as he reached the shallow part of the river he was pushed back.

Brock's heart began to pound. He had to get to that crossing. Had to get back across the stream. He wanted to go home. He wanted to take Heather and go home.

Once again, he was pushed back as soon as he reached it. Frustration and something akin to fear built up inside of him and he began to run outright. Ghostly whispers urged him on, making the hair rise on the back of his neck. He reached the crossing, and this time, he could practically feel the entities passing through him as they worked together to shove him back.

"Come on, ye bastards!" he screamed. Running full out, fighting the change so he could hold on to Heather, he pumped his legs as fast as they could go. His heart pounded and sweat trickled down his back.

Almost there. Almost there.

He was more than halfway there and this time, he would make it through them. He'd get through and get across the stream. If he could just get across the stream, everything would be okay.

A deep, hellish voice echoed through the trees, laughing at him. Laughing at his fear. Brock's heart stopped and his blood turned to ice in his veins. Cold, hard fear paralyzed him. He couldn't even scream…

Bolting upright from the ground he was lying on next to Heather, Brock startled awake with a terrified scream caught in his throat. His heart was pounding a mile a minute, his skin was rippling in anticipation of changing and a cold sweat covered him in spite of the nip in the air. The fire was almost burned out, and there was a pile of dry clothes folded next to it. Night was receding as a new day lightened the sky.

A dream...it was just a bad dream.

At least that's what he would tell himself.

CHAPTER 16

Heather, still in a barely half-conscious state, tried to discern what the hell it was she was hearing. There was a deep rumbling in her ear that didn't coincide with her body being rocked to and fro like a swing. No, not a swing, more like a hammock. A hammock made of the never-ending fog that she'd been stuck in for the past few days.

She tried to stretch her stiff bones, and that was when she felt the rigid bands of muscle under her back and knees.

Brock?

As she struggled to open her eyes, she became aware that she was being cradled again a warm, hard chest. Her left arm was bent at the elbow and tied tight to her side, and the sounds she was hearing was Brock's voice under her ear as he grumbled with frustration.

"Fookin' trees. If I dinna see one more fookin' tree in me life, I willna care!"

The brogue was out in full force. This couldn't bode well.

"And ghosts? O' all th' things? Are you fookin' kidding me?" He blew out an unsteady breath and mumbled, "Just a dream. Just a fookin' dream."

Curious as to what she'd missed, Heather finally managed to crack one eye open, then groaned as even the dim daylight caused her head to ache like someone was jackhammering at her brain.

"Sunshine?"

She groaned again, "Shhh. Put me down, Brock. You're going to hurt yourself."

The motion stopped and she was pulled in closer, her face tucked between his head and shoulder as he hugged her tight.

"Ah, sunshine. Thank th' gods yer awake. I was starting tae get worried."

His long hair tickled her nose and she tried to push away from him with her free arm, but he just held her tighter. Her ribs ached and her stomach rolled unpleasantly. "Please, put me down!" she rasped.

The desperation in her voice must have finally gotten through to him, for he carefully set her on her feet, then helped her down to the damp ground when her legs didn't seem to want to hold her. She leaned forward and closed her eyes, fighting down the nausea. She felt like she'd been hit by a train.

"Your bones seem tae be just aboot healed. I had tae set a few of them. I hope I didn't hurt you more than necessary. I tried tae be quick aboot it."

Still hunched over, she reached out blindly for his

hand. When she found him, she squeezed his fingers. "Thank you. I'll be okay. Just give me a minute."

Once the sick feeling had passed, she eased herself up into a sitting position to find Brock's bright blue eyes trained anxiously on her face. She offered him a weak smile. "You'd think us Faeries would be a little more waterproof."

"I don't think it was floating in the water that did you in, so much as the fall at the end of it."

Ah, good. He was calming down. She stretched her legs out in front of her and winced. Rubbing her healing calf, which was wrapped up in a makeshift splint, she looked around. "Where are we?"

Brock brushed away some pine needles with his foot and lowered himself down to the ground next to her. Pushing her hand away, he took over massaging her leg. "I think we're getting close to where I 'dropped' in. The water's receded quite a bit and I've been following the stream, which is now less like the Amazon and more like the Mississippi. I, uh, crossed at a shallow part to get us back on the right side of it, and I found one of my markers right before you woke up. I just don't know which one it is as it's the only one I've found, and the landscape, such as it is, is different now after all the flooding."

"How long have you been carrying me?" she asked.

He shrugged. "About twenty-six hours is my best guess."

She stared at him in mute horror. How were his arms anything but limp noodles by now? When she could speak again, she asked, "Why not just camp out somewhere until

I woke up? We still have a couple of days until our time is up."

He glanced down at her and clenched his jaw. "I'm ready to get out of here."

And away from her.

The words he didn't need to say bounced around her head. Her throat closed on a wave of sadness and all she could do was nod her agreement. But she didn't agree, not really. Not at all.

His hands stilled on her sore leg and he frowned with confusion when he saw the look on her face, then his eyes cleared as understanding dawned on him. He scooted over closer to her and tipped her face up to his with a finger under her chin. "I said I was ready to get out of this place, not away from you." His steady gaze bore into her own tear-filled one.

She turned her face away from him, not wanting him to see how much the thought of never seeing him again affected her. "That's kind of a done deal. Once we leave here, it'll be back to the real world for us. I'll go back to my people, and you'll go back to yours."

"No." His tone was firm.

Closing her eyes, she fought down the sliver of hope that was trying to work its way up into her heart. He'd only said 'no'. She didn't know what he was saying 'no' about. He could just mean that he wasn't going back to his people. It could have nothing to do with her.

Pulling her face back around and holding it there this time, he waited until he had her undivided attention. "I'm not losing you," he told her with his heart in his eyes. "I won't."

Okay. Maybe she could let herself feel a little bit of hope.

"But there are things you need to know about me, before I can ask you to give up everything to be with me."

"Things like what?" she asked.

Leaning back, he took a deep breath and looked around. "That's a long story to tell. Maybe we should keep walking…"

"Brock. What things?" She wasn't about to let him drop something like that and then expect her to just forget about it until later. "What things?" she insisted.

He pushed his hair back off of his face, gathering it together at his nape and letting it go again. Rubbing his palms on his thighs, he peeked over at her.

Heather waited for him to get his thoughts together, her stomach in knots again. Whatever he was about to tell her, it couldn't be as bad as her not telling him what she was.

Could it?

He cleared his throat. "Heather, I'm a lone wolf, a *siubhal.*" When she showed a lack of comprehension, he clarified, "I'm a wolf without a pack, because I was kicked out of the one I was in."

From the gravity in his voice, that must be serious indeed. She asked the obvious question. "Why?"

"Because I was accused of breaking one of the pack laws."

"What law?"

His jaw set in a stubborn line and he looked away.

Even not knowing what law he had broken, she had to ask, "Did you do it?"

He wrapped his arms around his knees and looked away. "I didn't deny it."

Something about his posture had her asking again, "But did you do it?"

This time, he looked straight at her. "I confessed."

"Oh." Somehow, Brock didn't strike her as a lawbreaker, be it pack law or made up rules in a Fae prince's game. But he'd confessed. He'd just said so himself.

"There's more," he said, interrupting her thoughts. "Once you've been kicked out of the pack, you're banned from ever returning anywhere near their territory, if you manage to survive the judgment against you."

"What do you mean? Survive?" Heather was having a hard time swallowing all of this.

"It's the way it is," he said without a trace of anger toward those who had done it to him. "I'm lucky I made it out of there alive. The rest of the pack beat me near to death, as is the custom, when our pack leader announced his decision. They left me where I fell. I honestly don't know how I survived. Most don't, and find it preferable to living with the shame of being exiled from your pack."

His eyes, which had taken on a far away look, snapped back to her. "I hold no anger toward them for what they did. My old pack master was good to me. He took me and my friend in when we were young and stupid and alone. Anyway, I thought you should know that about me before I ask you."

Heather's mind was still reeling. He'd been beaten? Had almost died? How had he managed to live through something like that? "Ask me what?" she wondered distractedly.

"I want to ask you to stay with me. After we get out of here. I want you to stay with me."

"Fae and shifters can't mate," she mumbled automatically, her mind still on everything he'd just told her.

Reaching for her hand, he clasped it between both of his larger ones. "I know they don't. And I know what I'm asking of you by even suggesting this. We'll both be outcasts, unable to ever be with our people. I'm used to that, and maybe it's not fair of me to ask you to join me in my exile, but…" He paused, playing with her fingers.

"But what?"

He sat up straighter, and gathered his courage. "I've always been fine being alone. I was alone for a long time before I found my pack, and I've been alone again for a few years now. But since I met you, I…you fill a hole in me that I didn't know was there."

He seemed to stop breathing as he waited for her reaction. She cocked an eyebrow at him. "I fill a hole?"

He blew out a frustrated breath and she bit back a smile. She could make it easy for him, and tell him that she couldn't give two shits about her so-called "people", other than her parents. But that would ruin all of her fun. And she was thoroughly enjoying watching him squirm.

Besides, there was still the matter of the law he'd broken. And what that would mean for them. Would there be more repercussions later? Was he just using her as a replacement for his lack of pack mates?

Logically, she knew this was a horrible idea. But how

often does a girl come across a male like him? And have him actually want to stick around?

"Sunshine…" The pained vulnerability in his voice pulled her from her thoughts. "I need you, so verra much. I haven't been able tae get you out of my head since the day I first saw you. I know I dinna deserve you, but I'm asking here. I'm asking you tae please think aboot staying with me. Now that I know you, now that I've had you, I dinna know how I ever lived without you." He held her eyes with his, and his shone with all of the feelings he was trying so hard to say. "I will protect you with my last breath from any who would dae you harm. I swear it."

Well, now, how the hell was she supposed to say no to that speech? Said with that sexy accent no less? No matter what he'd done or hadn't done in the past, she knew this male that was here before her now. Her body knew him. Her heart knew him.

"If you're planning on sweeping me off of my feet and taking me away to your castle to ravish me at your whim, you'd best get us the hell out of here first." She smiled at the shocked disbelief on his face.

"Is that a yes?" he asked with cautious hope forming in his beautiful eyes.

"That's a yes," she confirmed.

A roguish grin lit up his handsome features. "Ah, sunshine, if you weren't so black and blue, I would ravish you right now."

"I heal quite fast," she breathed, her body responding to the heat coming off of him.

But he laughed and shook his head. "Let's get home. Where we can shower and fill our bellies, and I can make love to you properly. In a bed. Without worrying about strange monsters or being boiled alive or…"

"Or what?"

"Nothing," he said quickly. Too quickly.

She tried not to pout as he got to his feet and helped her up. Bending over, he scooped her up into his arms again.

"I think I can walk," she told him, worried about the condition of his back after hauling her around for so long.

Kissing her on the temple, he just said, "Aye. I know you can. But I want to hold you."

And well, who could argue with that?

CHAPTER 17

Even though he knew he should be looking for the markers he'd left to lead them back to where the note had indicated, Brock couldn't take his eyes from the luscious female in his arms. Even covered in dried mud and bruises, she was the prettiest thing he'd ever set eyes on.

She must have felt him staring, for she peeked up at him from under her lashes and grinned.

He grinned back.

"What's that?" she asked, pointing to the right.

Tearing his eyes from her, he saw a piece of material hanging from a tree branch. About three feet away was another one. He looked down just in time. Another couple of steps and he would've fallen into the crater he'd left in the ground when he'd landed.

He could feel the excitement that must be shining from his eyes as he told her, "We're here!" Turning in a tight circle, he waited for something to happen.

"Are you sure this is the right spot?" she asked.

His heavy brows drew down into a frown as he carefully placed her on her feet, but he didn't let go of her. This time, they would go into the void together.

"I'm positive. I left those markers, and this is where I landed." He indicated the crack in the ground his body had made.

"You did that? And you didn't break anything?"

"I changed mid-air. My wolf form can take a lot more than my human body."

Heather started limping toward the crack to take a closer look, but he grabbed her arm.

"Stay with me. We don't know when we'll suddenly get sucked back again, and I want you to be with me."

She hung on to his hand. "Why were you alone?"

Brock studied the area. This had to be the right place. It was exactly how he'd left it less than five days ago, and he'd been given five days to get her back here. Maybe they'd go back on the fifth day? He suddenly realized she was staring at him, waiting for something, and he wracked his brain for what she'd said but couldn't remember. "What?"

"Why were you alone?"

He frowned. "I told you."

But she shook her head. "No, I mean before. Before you found your old pack. Why were you alone?"

"Oh, that. My parents died when I was very young. When I was eight, actually." Distracted, he stuck his free hand in his pocket, looking for the note he'd been left, but then remembered that it had been lost along with the coins when he'd lost his other clothes in the flood. He hoped they wouldn't be expected to pay their passage back with them.

"Didn't they belong to a pack? Didn't you have a family to take care of you?"

The sad tone of her voice finally got his attention. "Yes, we did. The pack was killed. Only my best friend and I survived. We were off playing by the loch when it happened. Oh," he smiled. "I should tell you that I grew up in Scotland. Which is how I know what heather smells like."

Her careful expression didn't change or give anything away. "Who killed your pack?"

His hand tightened around hers. She would find out sooner or later. "I was told later that they were Fae. They ambushed the pack near dusk, when they were busy getting meals together and children gathered. Lucian and I were never good at getting home on time. Lucky for us."

"Oh, my God." Tears filled her beautiful cognac-colored eyes. "How can you stand to be near me?"

He frowned. "*You* didn't do it." He stepped closer and pulled her into his arms. "It's okay. It was a long time ago."

She hid her face in his shirt and mumbled something that sounded like, "Butter peed on it!"

He laughed out loud. "What?"

Looking up at him in all seriousness, she said, "But my people did it!"

"You said they weren't your people. That your parents had taken you away and you grew up just like any other kid."

"They did, but..."

"But nothing. Were you there when it happened?"

"No…"

"Then why should I blame you?"

She sniffed and planted her face back in his shirt.

"So, let me ask you something. What else can you do besides move as fast as a vamp and shoot blue lightening from your fingers?"

She shrugged and wiped her teary face on his clean shirt. "I have no idea. I didn't even know that I could do that until it happened. Can we sit down?"

"Don't see why not. But let's stay as close to this spot as we can." He helped her sit against the closest tree trunk. "Are you cold?" The mist seemed to be getting heavier.

"No, I'm okay. I have a hot-blooded werewolf to keep me warm." She gave him a bit of a watery smile.

"Hey, that's enough of that. Let's talk about something else."

"How did you end up in that pack you were in if yours…was gone?"

Settling back next to her, he kept a firm grip on her hand, knowing from previous experience how quickly she could be sucked away from him. "Well, Lucian and I actually lived on our own for a few years. We had this secret fort down by the loch, and after we'd gone home and found out what had happened, we ran back there to hide. We ended up staying there for a long time. We collected water, and we fished for food or hunted nearby. And we had each other." He smiled fondly at the memories.

"But eventually, puberty hit and we got restless, so we ventured out. We were about thirteen when we came across the new pack. They took us in, helped us through our first shifts, and invited us to become full-fledged members when we were old enough to pass their tests. They'd been good to us, so we stayed."

He neglected to mention that it was because of him that Lucian had been allowed to stay. Lucian had never found a way to deal with his family's deaths, and he'd hit puberty with a vengeance, always getting into fights and causing trouble. Brock couldn't even count how many times he'd had to get between his friend and some other male to calm the waters.

As Lucian had gotten older, the females had really started to take notice of him. With his chiseled jaw, muscular physique, auburn hair, and intense grey eyes, they were drawn to him like bees to honey.

Even some of the mated females had a hard time staying away from him when he turned on the charm. Which meant Brock had spent most of his time making sure that Lucian stayed out of trouble. He needed the pack, whether he realized it or not. He needed them much more than Brock did.

Coming back to the present, he said, "So, back to you. Do I need to worry about you zapping me into another dimension whenever I piss you off?"

She laughed. "I don't think so. Only the most powerful of the Fae could pull off something like this. The rest of us are only good at parlor tricks."

No sooner had the words come out of her mouth then they heard a rustling in the tree limbs above them. Brock jumped to his feet and tilted his head back, alert to anything that may be coming for them through the fog.

Something thunk'd on a branch not ten feet above them, and Heather quickly struggled to her feet, out of the line of fire. A moment later, a golden coin fell to the ground at his feet.

"You've got to be fucking kidding me," he said in disbelief.

A second coin bounced off of Heather's shoulder to land in the grass and pine needles by her shredded up sneaker.

Brock stopped breathing as her eyes met his. He shook his head. "No. NO!" he shouted to the sky.

She laid her hand on his arm, "Brock…"

"NO," he gritted out. "I will not play this fookin' game anymore! No' anymore!!" His fists clenched tight at his sides, he walked out to the scarred ground where he'd landed, pulling Heather with him. "We are DONE, prince! Or whoever the hell ye are! Send us home. NOW!"

The air around them was still. No black voids opened up to suck them back to reality.

"Come on!" he shouted. "I followed yer fookin' rules. I did wha' the paper said. I have the girl! We're here, where I started. I even played yer fookin' game! Now hold up yer end o' the deal!"

Breathing hard, his hand gripped tight around Heather's wrist so he didn't lose her again. He waited… and waited…

"AHHHHHHHH!!!!!!" he screamed.

Heather wrapped her free arm around his waist as she pressed herself against his back. Releasing her wrist, he pulled her arms tighter around him as he fought his rising temper.

"Maybe we just toss the stupid coins," she suggested.

Brock gritted his teeth. She was right. They had to play the prince's stupid game. He knew there would be no getting them out of there without doing so. She tried to pull away, and after a moment, he let her. Bending down she picked up the coins and brought one to him, keeping one for herself.

"On the count of three," she said. "Ready?"

He gave her a barely perceptible nod.

"One, two...three."

They threw the coins in the air, both calling out, "Heads!" They looked at each other and smiled.

Heather's coin, thrown not quite as high as Brock's and unbeknownst to them, paused in mid-air. It seemed to hesitate, thinking, then very deliberately it turned to face the other way before falling back toward the ground.

They both looked back up just in time to catch their respective coins. Slapping them onto the backs of their opposite hands in unison, Brock swallowed nervously.

"One, two, three," Heather whispered, and they both removed their hands.

Brock nearly got light-headed with relief when he saw the prince's face staring back at him. With a wide grin, he looked up at Heather. She was staring down at the coin on the back of her hand, her face unreadable. He stepped closer to see her coin.

An etching of a pine tree, meticulously done, shone deep yellow against her pale skin. Heather raised uneasy eyes to his as Brock grabbed the coin from her hand and chucked it into the crack in the ground. When he turned back around, Heather was staring at him in outright horror. He took both of her hands in his. "It's okay, sunshine. I've got you. Nothing is going to happen."

"It already is," she told him.

Confused, he pulled her closer, terrified that she was going to get ripped from his arms at any second.

CHAPTER 18

Heather knew Brock's arms were around her, but she couldn't feel them. She was too numb with fear. They were coming.

"Heather...Sunshine...what is it? What do you see?" Brock's voice came at her as if from a long distance away.

She tried to answer him. Her mouth opened, but her throat was closed tight.

They were coming. The bad ones. They were here. And they were coming for her.

"Heather, please talk to me!" Brock pulled back, gripping her by the chin and tilting her face up his. His eyes were wide and scared, his nostrils flaring as if he could smell her fear. "What is happening?"

"They're coming," she managed to whisper.

"Who's coming?"

Her throat worked as she tried to speak. He gave her a gentle shake.

"Who is coming?"

Out of the corner of her eye, she saw figures emerge from the mist to stand just inside the trees to their left. Adrenaline suddenly rushed through her body. "The bad ones. And they're here." Staying within the circle of his arms, she turned to face the Fae creatures.

Brock followed her gaze. "I don't see anything. Heather! I don't see anything!"

Stepping in front of him, she took up a protective stance. "They're here, trust me."

"What do they want?"

She didn't know how she knew. Maybe it was instinct, maybe it was the way their hollowed, orange eyes kept moving back and forth from her to him, becoming distinctly hostile when they landed on her werewolf. "They want me. And they want to kill you."

Brock swung his eyes around, searching for this new threat. "Why can't I see them?"

She shook her head slightly. "I don't know. But I can. Just stay behind me."

A low growl rumbled behind her. "I will no' cower behind my female and leave her tae defend me."

"It doesn't look like you've got much of a choice, big guy." She could see them all now: Six males, all smaller than Brock, but no less lethal. They were dressed in human clothes, jeans or other casual pants, boots and long-sleeved, fitted tees. But their sunken eyes, thin, twitchy bodies, and shaved, tattooed heads ended the resemblance there.

They looked like they all suffered from a severe case of

meth addiction and hadn't had their fix in a long time. Which, she supposed, was kinda true.

She faced off against them, doing her best to ignore Brock and focus on the things in front of her. Her fingers tingled and she shook out her hands, trying to get the blood circulating. Although the way her heart was pounding, she didn't know how any part of her body wasn't receiving its fair share of her blood supply.

She was utterly terrified, but was trying hard not to show it. She didn't know how to fight! Especially not against a mystical being.

The one in front with the tattoo that dropped down into a V onto his forehead, suddenly appeared mere inches from her. Grabbing a handful of her thick hair, he pulled back, forcing her into an awkward half backbend. Holding her that way with one leanly muscled arm, he leaned down and smelled her.

"You stink like heather," he spit out. His breath smelled like decayed meat.

She reached up with both hands and tried to dislodge his hand from her hair, but his grip was like an iron band. Brock had his hands on her waist and shoulders, trying to pull her upright as he let out a stream of curse words, but he was only hurting her more. "Brock, let go! You're hurting me!"

He immediately dropped his hands, only to start pacing back and forth helplessly next to them. He never took his glowing eyes from her.

"V" gave her hair a good yank, and she winced. "I said, you stink like heather."

"So I've been told," she squeaked.

"Who are you talking tae? Where are they?" Brock roared.

Her eyes went to the Fae male of their own accord and Brock immediately took a swing in that direction. The male ducked just in time, almost dropping Heather to the ground.

"Control your dog, or we will kill him slowly and painfully while you watch." Blotchy colors radiated from his irises, the dark circles under his eyes making them stand out like strobe lights.

"Fuck you," Heather told him quite succinctly.

Smiling and showing off rotten teeth, he swung his arm backward, tossing her across the crevice in the ground to land hard in front of his posse.

Brock threw his head back and howled. Heather heard the crack of breaking bones and the moist, slushy sound of muscle tissue ripping and covered her ears and closed her eyes. Curling herself into a ball, she stayed like that until another howl rent the air, followed by loud snarls and the snap of his teeth.

She opened her eyes just in time to see boots clear her prone body as the remaining five Fae jumped over and around her to help their friend. Reaching up, she snagged one of them by the ankle. "Oh no, you don't, asshole."

He fell flat on his face, and she wasted no time getting to her feet. She was ready when he got up. Ripping off her sling and ignoring the deep throbbing in her leg, she sank into a low fighting stance and waited for him to make the first move.

Running his crazy eyes over her, he assessed the threat as he wiped the dirt off of his mouth.

Heather heard grunts of pain coming from Brock. She wanted to check on him, but didn't dare take her eyes from her opponent. He cocked his head at her.

"Really? A fist fight? This is what you're doing?" Leaning forward, he said in a stage whisper, "I can suck the soul from your body before you get in a single punch."

So she kicked him with a basic front kick. Hard. Right in the balls.

Both of his hands cupped his nether regions to protect them, too late, and Heather took advantage of his position to land an uppercut right in the jaw. His head whipped back and she danced out of the way as he roared with rage at her. Stuttering, weak blue lights shot from his fingers in her general direction, but came short of actually hitting her.

She felt strangely calm as he screamed at her. When she got tired of hearing it, she nailed him with a left hook and followed it up with a spinning kick to the kidney. Hopping on top of him, she followed him to the ground as he fell. Placing both hands on either side of his head, she felt that same electricity flow through her fingers. The volts burst through his skull and into his head, killing him instantly.

Heather stared down at him as she slowly removed her hands, quite unable to believe what she had just done. A loud crack and the sound of a tree falling pulled her out of her trance, and she glanced up to see Brock's prone body lying on the ground underneath the broken top half of a fallen pine tree. V and his cohorts were circling around the wolf. As she watched, one of them kicked him in the ribs so hard, his limp form lifted a foot off the ground.

Rage filled her; so pure and white that she was standing between them and her wolf before she'd even realized that she moved. With a scream, she grabbed the kicker's head in her hands and smashed his face into her knee. Deep blue streams of pulsating electricity flew from her fingers as she threw him to the side and went after the next guy.

Her fist connected with his nose with a satisfying crunch. Spinning around, she kicked out, catching the shorter one flashing up behind her. She hadn't even realized he was there. He fell back with a grunt, landing on top of Brock.

She only watched long enough to see her wolf's jaws clamp down on the male's throat before she turned to finish off the guy whose nose she'd broken. Her eyes widened as her fury receded, and she experienced her first flash of true terror.

While V stood off to the side watching with a satisfied smirk on his face, the bloody one lunged for her. His mouth was open wide and his eyes were crazy, and she froze, paralyzed with fear. Or was it?

She felt the beginning of a pull inside of her, like someone had a hold of her spine and was trying to yank it out through her mouth. Fighting the sensation, she dropped to the ground just as he reached her. Planting her feet directly on his chest she rolled backwards, using his own momentum to send him flying over her head. Twisting around, she came up behind him and slammed both palms onto the sides of his head. He was dead as quickly as his friend.

Kickboxing ruled.

Breathing hard, she jumped to her feet, prepared to take on V. But he was gone. She searched the area all around them, but he'd just disappeared.

A strong gust of wind blew her hair around her face as she made her way over to Brock. He was still lying on his side where he'd landed, and his jaws were still clamped around the Fae's throat. Muted eyes widened in fear as she approached, and in spite of the teeth embedded into his neck, he started struggling to free himself.

Brock grunted as the guy landed an elbow into his tender belly, but didn't release his hold. With a snarl that would make her wolf proud, Heather held her hands out in front of her. Blue light crackled and hissed at her fingertips as she slowly walked toward him. A second later, he stopped struggling as she ended him.

Grabbing him by his clothes, Heather rolled him off of her wolf, dragging him as far away as she could. Brock watched her before letting his head fall back to the ground. Crawling over to him, she ran her hands over his head and side, searching for injuries. He whined quietly when she hit a rib that was sore, and again when she felt down his left leg.

"What should I do?" she asked him, but he didn't even crack open an eye.

His breathing had calmed considerably. Heather was beginning to wonder if he had passed out when his body twisted backward. He yelped as it was flung forward again.

Scooting back to give him room, she closed her eyes and covered them with her hands for good measure. Tears ran down her cheeks as she listened to his obvious pain, made worse by his injuries. When he was quiet again except for his heavy breathing, she cracked her fingers open and peeked through.

He lay on his back, gloriously naked. One large hand reached out to her and she took it within her own two hands. Walking on her knees, she got as close to him as she could. His side was already turning a nice purple color.

"What can I do?" she asked him again.

Pulling her hands toward his mouth, he kissed her fingers. "You can grab my clothes over there and help me get dressed."

Looking around, she did indeed find his clothes. He must have yanked them off before he changed. She brought them over and helped him sit up, and then stand. Though she probably wasn't much help, still limping as she was. Now that the adrenaline rush was gone, her leg was aching like a bitch. "What about your ribs? And your arm?"

Though his pain and exhaustion showed on his face, he shrugged it off nonchalantly. "I've had worse. I think the arm is just fractured anyway. It'll be fine in an hour."

"And the ribs?"

"Yeah, probably just bruised."

He kept giving her funny looks as she helped him get dressed, like he couldn't decide whether to be proud or frightened of her.

She scowled. "Quit looking at me like that. It's still me."

"I was quite unaware that my delicate little flower was such a bad ass." He grinned and bent over to tie his boots.

Standing up again, he tossed his hair out of his face. "I will endeavor to never make you angry at me."

"Well, don't do anything stupid, and I won't have to zap you." She stared at him, dead serious, until he started to fidget. Then she rolled her eyes. "Really, dude? The big, bad wolf is afraid of a little faerie dust?"

Dropping his head, he stared at the ground, then suddenly swooped her up off of her feet and threw her over his shoulder. "Nah. You don't scare me, sunshine." He ignored her screeching and smacked her on the bottom, then gave it a healthy squeeze. "God, I love your ass." His palm was so big it covered one entire cheek.

"Brock! Put me down! Right now, you overgrown dog!"

He ignored her ranting and carried her back over to the crack in the earth. Giving her another sharp slap (that if she were to be honest, she kind of liked), he said, "Shhh. Listen."

Heather used her good arm as leverage and pushed the top half of her body up. Shoving her hair out of her face, she listened.

The wind was moaning through the trees, and it sounded like it was picking up speed. Brock spun in a circle, making her dizzy, and she was about to fuss at him to hold still when she realized that it wasn't Brock that was moving. It was the world around them.

She felt herself falling and gripped the back of his shirt before realizing that he was lifting her off of his shoulder.

"If I start to change," He had to yell now over the howling wind. "Just try to stay with me!" Wrapping her in his strong arms, he linked his hands behind her. "Hang on!"

Heather buried her face in his shirt and grabbed a hold of the waistband of his pants. His heart thundered under her ear, mimicking her own frantic heartbeat. She felt herself being pulled backwards.

"Here we go! Hang on, sunshine!" he yelled in her ear.

His arms were like steel bands around her. A force gripped her around the middle and she screamed as she was pulled backwards.

Brock's roar joined her as he was pulled along with her, the only thing holding her to him being his own force of will. Together, they tumbled into the darkness.

CHAPTER 19

"What the actual fook?"

Brock froze at the sound of the all too familiar voice, a hot flash of fear heating his skin. It couldn't be.

A quick glance over his shoulder confirmed that the voice did indeed belong to the person he thought it did, and his heart stalled out in his chest before picking back up to pound rapidly behind his ribs. There was only one reason that he would be here. And it wasn't going to end well for either of them.

Turning back to Heather, he took her face in his large hands and whispered sincerely, "I'm so sorry. I should've told you everything." Then he released her and turned around to face the ugliness of the past that he'd been running from since he'd met her.

"Brock? Is tha' you?" Lucian, the male that had once been his best friend and only family, stood to the side of the kitchen with both a question and a warning in his stormy grey eyes. "What the fook am I doing here?"

Not a "Hey, buddy!" Not a "Good to see ya!" He hadn't changed a bit, Brock was sad to see. Still the same auburn-haired, pretty-boy looks. Still the same selfish, cocky attitude.

Standing beside Lucian was Cedric, the pack leader he had gone to visit to seek permission to stay in Seattle. He stared at Brock with the icy intelligence and calm, powerful presence that allowed him to retain the position he was in. It was quite obvious that they'd both been "invited" here the same way he and Heather had just arrived.

Why was Lucian with Cedric?

"Oh good! Our guests are here," the Fae prince crowed with delight. "Heather dear, come sit over here by me." He patted the seat next to him, a kitchen stool that he'd pulled up to the counter. After a searching look at Brock, which he couldn't answer, she limped over with obvious reluctance and sat down.

"How was your trip?" he asked Brock with genuine curiosity.

Brock watched her join the prince, half expecting him to hand her some popcorn for the show. "It was…unexpected," he answered, and then turned to the prince's "guests". He lowered his head with respect, though not as far as he would have if he were a member of their pack, and greeted the alpha.

"Cedric." Straightening up, he speared Lucian with a resentful stare, all of the undeserved violence and loneliness of the past years converging inside of him. "Lucian."

He spit out the name of the male that was once a brother to him.

Cedric gave Brock a slight nod in greeting, glancing between him and Lucian with curious, narrowed eyes. He then turned to the Fae prince, the slight clenching and unclenching of his jaw the only visible sign that he was at all frazzled by finding himself in someone else's kitchen so unexpectedly. "Now that ye 'ave us here, who are ye and what is it exactly that we can dae for ye?" he asked in his heavy Scottish brogue as he crossed his heavy arms over his wide chest. "Ye interrupted my binge watching on Netflix, and I do nae appreciate it."

"I'm so glad you asked! And I will get to the answer of that question soon, I promise," the prince responded glee-fully, then held up one finger as his expression became serious and just a bit morose. "But first, let me briefly fill you in on why I interrupted your *busy* lives to bring you here to my expensive, albeit humble, home."

"Is that nae wha' I just asked?" Cedric looked around at the others in the room for confirmation.

The prince waved a hand in Brock's direction. "You know this wolf."

It wasn't a question, but after a pause, Cedric answered anyway. "Aye, I dae, but nae well. We met only briefly upon his arrival in my territory. I got th' impression he was a braw lad."

Brock felt his face burn at the slight tone of consterna-tion in the alpha's voice. It was barely discernible, but it was there. Heather's eyes were drilling holes in him, but he refused to look at her. He couldn't. He could only imagine what she must be thinking.

Pushing his long hair back away from his forehead, he half wondered where the prince was going with this by bringing Lucian here and outing him in front of the alpha. But he was afraid he knew.

The question was: Would he give him the answers that he was searching for? And if he did, would it be worth it to see his old friend brought down a notch or two? Having the truth out in the open would salvage Brock's reputation, possibly even open up a spot for him in his old pack again—he glanced at Cedric—or get him an offer to join a new one. But would it be worth it? Would it make him feel any better to ruin Lucian's life? Though he missed the connection of having a pack, Brock was strong enough to survive as a *siubhal.* Was Lucian?

Brock knew the answer to that was a most definite no. It would destroy him.

The prince continued, "This wolf has been going through a series of tests, of sorts. You see, in spite of the perils of such an act, he has his cap set on my daughter here, but we needed to be certain that not only are their feelings for each other genuine, but that he is worthy of being the mate of someone such as she."

"She is nae a wolf," Cedric stated needlessly and with a final "there is nothing more to discuss" tone.

"No," the prince confirmed. "She is something much more."

Cedric looked around Lucian as he studied her with mild curiosity, his dark ponytail sliding over his shoulder. He automatically flipped it back again, and asked, "What dae this 'ave to dae with me? Or Lucian?"

The prince directed his next question to the young

wolf standing next to his alpha. "Lucian, you were Brock's friend once, correct? Practically his only family?"

Brock waited for him to deign to give the Fae prince his attention. In typical Lucian fashion, he kept his eyes on some distant point until Cedric reached over and smacked him on the shoulder like an errant teenager. His head snapped around and he glared at his pack master for a brief second before remembering who it was that he was glowering at.

He shoved his hands into the front pockets of his jeans. "Sorry," he said flippantly to Cedric before giving the Fae prince his attention. "Wha' was that?"

The prince narrowed his eyes at him and repeated his question. "You are Brock's friend, are you not?"

"Why should I tell ye anything?"

"Because," the prince said with a less than tolerant tone. "I asked."

"Just answer him, lad," Cedric ordered. "Afore ye get us into a situation."

"Aye," he answered mulishly with the briefest of glances at Brock. "I was."

He could see the nervousness in his old friend's eyes, hiding behind the cloak of the arrogant demeanor that he'd been wearing for the world in general ever since their parents had died. Lucian had always been an ass, and most people didn't care for him or his personality. But they had grown up together, inseparable since they were nothing but young pups. They'd gone through their first change together, their first experiences with girls together, had learned to hunt together and had fought their way into their first pack together when they'd come of age. Brock knew him better than anyone, and he knew that his outward attitude hid a kind, but insecure young male on the inside. But that didn't make it any easier to forgive him.

"You are no longer friends then?" the prince asked innocently.

As if he didn't know.

Lucian crossed his arms in a defensive gesture and shook his head.

"Why is that?" He looked genuinely confused.

Lucian fidgeted under the prince's steady gaze, sticking his hands back in his pockets and shifting his weight from foot to foot. "He left our old pack."

One silver eyebrow lifted in question. "'Left' your pack?"

Lucian glanced at Cedric, but received no help from that corner. Brock wondered what he'd told his new pack master about his past, because it was obvious now why Cedric was here. Was this crazy Fae actually trying to help him by exposing Lucian in front of his new alpha?

Lucian crossed his arms in front of him in a defensive gesture and lifted his chin. "Aye. He was kicked out."

"Ah yes. I remember it well." The prince tapped his finger against his chin, staring off into the distance.

Brock stared at him in confusion. He remembered it? What the hell was he talking about?

The prince glanced over at Heather, who hadn't torn her eyes away from Brock this entire time, and nodded in mock sympathy. He patted her hand with his and turned his attention to Cedric. "He was not only kicked out, but he was beaten to within an inch of his long life. Isn't that the normal way of it with you canines?"

Brock heard Heather's intake of breath and his own lungs tightened in response, making it hard for him to breathe. Her concern warmed his insides, but she wouldn't be so sympathetic toward him when she found out why it had happened.

"The infraction he committed was severe," the prince continued without waiting for Cedric to answer. "They only did what was required for a crime of such severity. Is that not so?"

Cedric stared at him calmly, refusing to rise to the bait. "I would nae know, as I don't ken what he did."

"As a matter of fact, he did something so shameful and unforgivable…" the prince continued as if he hadn't spoken. Leaning forward toward the alpha, he divulged this shameful secret like he was gossiping with a girlfriend. "That he had to be ousted from his own pack."

Cedric was looking a little wary now as he eyed the Fae prince. "Aye. I got tha' part."

Brock watched the proceedings with a growing feeling of unease. Perhaps he'd been wrong. The bastard wasn't trying to help him; he was exposing *him*, not Lucian. He tightened his jaw. This was such bullshit. This stuff was in his past. It had nothing to do with him now, or with him wanting to be with Heather.

The prince caught his eye and smirked. Brock ground his teeth together. This was just a fucking game to him. He'd never had any intention of allowing him to be with Heather, and this final scene was just his way of ensuring that she would turn against him, since he'd proven himself worthy in every other way during his sick little game. After everything he'd just gone through, everything they'd shared, he thought he had Brock by the balls.

Well, he had a surprise for this asshole faerie. He met his accusatory stare head on, and refused to let the weight of his shame weigh him down. Instead, he stood tall and with his head held high, because he had nothing to be ashamed of. And soon, everyone here would know it.

"Whit was it exactly tha' Brock was accused of?" Cedric finally asked.

With an exaggerated wink at Brock, the prince turned to the large alpha leader and announced in an overly loud stage whisper, "He *attacked* one of the mated females in the pack. He forced himself upon her and got her with child."

Brock heard Heather's sharp intake of breath, but he still refused to look at her. He didn't want to see the look on her face. Not just yet. Instead, he turned to look at Lucian, searching for something, anything. Some small sign of remorse, or gratitude, or…*something*…to make him rethink what he was about to say.

But when Lucian glanced over at him, there was nothing. Not one sign of emotion. The corners of his mouth turned up in a smirk as he turned away, confident that Brock would never expose him after all of this time.

So that was the way it was gonna be? The last lingering remnants of uncertainty left him; along with any misplaced feelings of loyalty he'd had for his childhood friend.

"Is there anything you would like to say for yourself, Brock?" the prince asked.

"Actually, there is," Brock stated firmly. Lucian stiffened and narrowed his eyes in warning. Returning the warning look for look, he opened his mouth to tell them the truth of what had really happened, but a flurry of movement caught his attention. The words he'd been about to speak withered and died in his throat as a stunning brunette woman came timidly down the hall and joined the group. A young child clung to her hand. A boy. With blonde hair and blue eyes and chubby cheeks.

Brock looked from the boy to his mother. Her eyes were wide, silently pleading with him not to say anything. Thomas, his old pack master, stepped up beside her. He gave Brock a small, relieved smile before spotting Lucian across the room. The smile instantly fell from his face.

Brock followed his gaze over to Lucian to see his reaction to this new development. His old friend didn't even glance at the woman and child, or at Thomas, and appeared bored with the entire proceeding.

Cedric was outwardly calm and hard to read, as he'd been this entire time. Only the slight sheen of disappointment in his eyes when he looked at Brock gave away any indication of how he was feeling about all of this.

"Thomas!" The prince's voice boomed across the room. "How are you, my old friend? I hope you've held things together since I've been gone?"

Holy fucking hell.

Memories flashed by at lightening speed. Brock and Lucian as part of their old pack. The new "advisor" that showed up out of nowhere. The unrest in the pack getting worse the moment he'd arrived. And how he'd been the one that had pushed for Brock's trial.

He'd looked different then, but the boots…he still wore

the same fucking silver-tipped boots. *That's* what had been trying to trigger his memory.

Thomas nodded at the prince, but didn't return the greeting.

"Mommy? Can I go see Uncle Lucian?" A small, excited voice cut through the tension in the room.

"Not just yet, sweetheart." The brunette woman murmured. Her heart was in her eyes as she stared at Lucian. Lucky for her, her pack master couldn't see it.

"But why? I *misses* him. He never comes visit us like he said. It makes my heart sad." His bottom lip stuck out in an adorable pout and he crossed his little arms over his narrow chest.

Brock caught the flash of pain that crossed his old friend's features at the child's honest words, right before he quickly donned his mask again. But it was enough. Enough to give him pause.

Closing his eyes, he wanted to scream with the unfairness of it all, but he knew he couldn't say what he wanted to say now. If for no other reason than that he couldn't destroy the lives of the woman and child. If he opened his mouth now and told them she hadn't been attacked, the woman would be tried for breaking pack law, just as he had been. And just like him, she would be found guilty, beaten, and (if she lived) ostracized from the pack. The child would be forced to watch his mother's downfall, and unless a compassionate, childless couple adopted him, would live his life as an orphan of the pack. Forever carrying the shame of the circumstances of his birth.

Steeling himself for what he knew he had to do, he finally made himself look at Heather. She was staring at the woman and child, her forehead wrinkled in confusion. It didn't take but a few moments for the confusion to be replaced by an expression of utter devastation.

Letting his eyes roam over her delicate features, so very precious to him, he tried again to memorize every detail: Her cognac eyes, slightly tilted at the corners like she was always about to laugh, now staring at him full of denial; her soft, chestnut hair that fell around them like a curtain when she leaned forward to kiss him as she was riding him with abandon; her soft breasts and rounded arms and full hips and thighs that cradled him so perfectly when she pulled him down to her…

The prince turned back to him and waited expectantly. Everyone was waiting for him to finish what he'd been about to say. He ignored them all except for Heather. She'd want nothing to do with him now. How could she?

No. She knew him well enough now. She wouldn't believe this bullshit. She wanted to be with him. She would know that all of this wasn't as it seemed. She would know better than to believe the crazy one sitting next to her. She would give him a chance to explain before she condemned him.

But when her eyes met his, they were full of accusations and mistrust. As he saw the shadows of her dawning comprehension darken her eyes, he had to bite his tongue so he wouldn't blurt out that it was all a fucking lie. That he'd been trying to protect his friend. And that now he needed to protect the woman and her innocent child.

Instead, he allowed his temper to take over. He was angry that she would believe something so low of him, angry that he was being put into this position *again*. He gnashed his teeth together and his chin tilted in defiance, disguising the pain that was flooding through him.

With one last glance at the mother and child, he announced with a forced steadiness in his voice, "It's true. I copulated with this female forcefully and behind her husband's back, and she bore my illegitimate child."

The Fae prince sat back in his chair, surprise and something akin to admiration flashing across his features.

Heather's face, on the other hand, crumbled in pain as her eyes went from him to the woman and child and back again.

He looked away, not needing to see any more. The shame and humiliation that he had kept simmering beneath the surface burned through him. Gritting his teeth, he glanced up at the woman and child. Her eyes were filled with grateful tears. They spoke the words she couldn't say. He gave her a tight nod.

Brock turned to leave, but then swallowed the few pieces that were left of his pride and walked over to stand in front of Heather. "I'm sorry I wasn't honest with you and that you had to find out this way. I wish I were a male worthy of you." He caught her eyes with his own. "You mean more to me than you know. I sincerely hope you have a long and happy life. All I ask is that, perhaps, you think of me once in a while, and know that I will *never* forget you." Turning on his heel, he managed to keep his head high until he'd gotten out the door and far enough away from them all that they couldn't see or hear him.

Wandering out onto the street, he headed right, back toward the airport. There was nothing here for him now. Heather would be staying here with her people. He would go back to Dalian. Back to his life as a *siubhal*. Back to his life hunting those fucking possessed vampires or whatever else he could find to keep him occupied.

He made it to the end of the street before the weight of all that had happened the past week came crashing down on him. He stumbled, fell to his knees in the middle of the dark street, and let the emotions roll through him. The feeling of loss was so strong it stole his breath, and he gasped for air around the aching hole punctured through his chest. Pictures of Heather's face flashed through his mind: Her head thrown back in passion…her eyes laughing up at him…her brow furrowed stubbornly when she defied him.

His palms could still feel her warm skin. He could still smell her woman's scent. Could still remember her taste. He wondered how long it would take for all of that to fade, little by little, until he couldn't feel her with him anymore. Until he couldn't remember her smile.

He could turn around. He could go back. Tell them the truth. Straighten everything out…

But no, he'd done the right thing. Everyone had their crosses to bear. This would be his. For the child's sake.

Heather sat in the heavy silence of the room, tears slipping silently down her cheeks. No one had moved or spoken since Brock had walked out. She felt like she'd just been through a bad episode of Survivor. She was dirty, tired, and she hurt like a bitch, both inside and out.

She studied the woman still standing quietly just inside the doorway, trying to keep the green eyed monster at bay and failing miserably. She was the most gorgeous creature Heather had ever seen. Short, choppy, black hair perfectly framed an elfish face. Large, dark eyes dominated her features, almost drawing your attention from her perfectly formed full lips, but not quite. Tight jeans and a clingy shirt accentuated a small hourglass figure. Heather felt like a big, fat hippo just being in the same room with her.

That was the kind of woman Brock should be with. One that was just as beautiful as he was. She couldn't blame him for wanting to be with her. But this whole "forced" business? Yeah, that was a crock of shit. Brock was the kindest, most gentle and protective male she'd ever met. He would never force himself on a woman. He wouldn't need to. Any woman in her right mind would want to be with him.

Next, her attention was drawn to the adorable child next to her, digging at the floor with the toe of his shoe. He was just as beautiful as his mother, only with lighter skin, hair, and features.

She was a fool. It was stupid of her to ever think that a man like him would want someone like her.

I will never forget you.

Another tear slipped down her face as she remembered what he'd just told her. That was kind of him to do that, to say that stuff. So that she didn't feel like a *complete* idiot.

"That did not turn out as I had expected."

The words came from the silver-haired male sitting next to her. His fingers were tapping on the arm of his chair, his expression lost in thought.

"Yeah, well, if you're done with me," she began as she started to get down from the stool. She just wanted to go home: Home to her own apartment, with her own shower, and her own lonely bed. Maybe she'd get a dog. Or a cat. Or five. Cats were easier. You didn't have to walk them.

But he grabbed her hand and pulled her back down. "Oh no, dear. I'm nowhere near done with you. Stay awhile, why don't you?"

She felt herself being pushed back into her chair, although no one was touching her. Finished with this loon and his amusements, her temper snapped. Swinging her arm to the side, she pushed away his control with a force of will she wasn't aware she had and stood up again. "Fuck you, prince whatever-the-hell-your-name-is. I'm going home. Far away from you and your Wonderland games."

"Nada," he said.

She rolled her eyes. "What? I don't speak Spanish."

"That's my name. Prince Nada. *Your* prince, Heather Knight."

"You're not my prince."

"Oh, but I am. Whether you like it or not. Now please," he indicated the empty chair next to him. "Please. Sit down and hear me out. Then if you would still like to leave, I won't stop you."

She knew she shouldn't trust him, but as she was too tired to fight her way out of there, she did as he asked. Since he'd been so polite about it and all.

"Wha' aboot us?" Cedric asked. "I cannae see that our presence here is still needed now that yer little show is over."

The prince smiled at him. "You are correct, good sir. I will send you all home." He lifted his hand, and a strong wind whistled through the kitchen, blowing Heather's hair into her face. The floor rumbled as he snapped his fingers and a large, dark chasm opened up behind Thomas, the woman, and the child. With a "whoosh", they were gone, the child's dwindling scream echoing through the room.

He swung his arm toward his other guests, but then he paused. "Oh! Just one thing, Mr. Kincaid. The werewolf - Brock Hume. He is all that you think he is, and is worthy of being offered a place in your pack. Believe it or not, he's proven himself today more so than even I had ever thought possible."

"I dinna ken aboot that. No' after what I just heard."

"You may want to ask the male standing next to you what he thinks about the matter before you pass a final judgment." With a snap, they were gone.

"Please don't do that to me again," Heather begged. "I barely survived the first time. I'd much rather be squished into coach on a regular old plane with everyone else."

Rising elegantly from his chair, Prince Nada paced away from her, his hands clasped behind his back. He walked the length of the kitchen and back, his head lowered in thought. When he made it back to her, he smiled and nodded to himself before pulling his chair around to face her and taking a seat.

"Forgive me for my bit of fun that I had with you two. I'm sure there was a less…disruptive…way to find out what I needed to know about you both. But I am getting old, and with trying to stay under the human's radar and all of that, I don't have much fun anymore."

"What exactly *was* the point of all of this?" she asked, waving her hand in front of her to encompass him, the house, and the entire past week.

Prince Nada gave her an intense stare, watching her closely as he carefully chose his next words. "It was…for many reasons. The coins were just for fun. But mostly, it was about you. By the way," he said in an aside. "Be glad you didn't find out what the losing coin would have brought on when you two were at the spring."

She didn't even want to think about that. "Me?" she squeaked. "It was about *me*?"

"Yes, you."

Heather sat back in her chair and rubbed her forehead. "Before a few days ago, you didn't even know I existed. How can this be about me?"

"Oh, I knew that you existed. I just didn't know where you were. My powers are great, but unfortunately, they are limited. And after all of this time, daughter, I needed to know if all of those years you'd lived as a human had ruined you."

"Why do you keep calling me daughter? I'm not your daughter."

"But you are. You are all my children. This entire Fae tribe. Mine to enjoy, and mine to watch over. We are connected." He hooked his two index fingers together and a wistful smile saddened his features. "This world used to belong to us. Our people used to frolic together in the flowers, sleep in the trees under the stars, and eat the food that grew naturally from the ground. We used to take care of the plants, the forests, and the animals. Other than a minor squabble or two over a female or a crop, we lived in peace and harmony with everything around us."

"We still live like that, only with a few more modern conveniences."

But he shook his head. "No. It was different. We didn't have to hide what we were. Even when the humans started multiplying, invading more and more of our world, we were able to live in harmony with them. We had a little fun with them at times, but nothing that would hurt them." He heaved a deep sigh. "That is, until someone, somewhere, decided that humans were more than just interesting creatures we could harmlessly play with."

A frown wrinkled his brow. "I still don't know who it was exactly that started all of the feeding off of the humans." He waved his hand around like he was fanning away an unpleasant odor. "But no matter. It was done. They told someone, who told someone, who told someone. Next thing you know, we had an epidemic on our hands. Our people were addicted. Oh, not all of us," he was sure to point out. "But enough. The humans became frightened of us, with good reason. They began to hunt the Fae. Good ones, bad ones, it didn't matter. They didn't know the difference."

"I still don't understand what this has to do with me," Heather said.

Resting his elbows on his knees, he leaned closer to her. "Because they're coming."

Heather cocked an eyebrow. "Who is coming?"

"The ones that steal the souls."

"I thought they were locked away somewhere? Like in some other dimension or something?" She frowned. "Wait a minute. So, where the hell did I just spend the last week?"

He chose to only answer her first question. "They are. They are. But that portal is going to open, and soon. And then they'll be out, running amok amongst the good people of this world. And I'm afraid that this time, it will be the end for the humans. The bad ones will be like rabid beasts when they come out of there."

"Well," Heather cast about for something to ease the very real concern she saw on his face. "Can't you just put them back in there?"

An ecstatic smile lit up his eyes and spread across his

face. "Yes! And we will! But it will take all of us. Fae, were-wolves…everyone. And you, you will help us too."

"I will?"

"You must. It's all up to you, my dear. You are the key."

Heather fought the urge to roll her eyes. What a drama queen this dude was. "You lost me again there, prince."

"You and the wolf, Brock. You two will bring us together again to fight the life-takers. And now that you are coming into your magic again, you will be a great asset to us." A rainbow of colors began to come and go in the irises of his eyes, like a freaky kaleidoscope spinning inside his skull. "With you as his mate, the wolves will feel honor bound to help us again. And they must! They must defend us! This war, daughter…this war is going to be so much worse than the last time. These Fae have been locked away for hundreds of years, they must be completely stir crazy by now. If not from boredom, than from the withdrawals they are most certainly still suffering from…"

She held up a hand to stop his blathering. "There's just one problem here. Well, two actually. One: I am not Brock's mate. In case you didn't notice, he left me here. And judging from the woman he was with before, I'm not exactly his type. Surprise, surprise." She fought down the acid that rose in her throat to admit it out loud. "And two: He doesn't belong to a pack. He's a sib…something. Or sub…something. He's a lone wolf. Kicked out. Banished. Why would any of the others band together with him to help him fight our war?"

But the Fae prince just smiled. "The first concern is not even a concern. He is madly in love with you. Or he will be, very soon. For now, he lusts after only you. You are meant to be," he whispered.

Heather's eyes flashed up to him.

"And the second," he continued. "Is already in the works. Brock will not be a lone wolf for much longer."

"He loves me?" she breathed. Then she narrowed her eyes. "How do you know this?"

Prince Nada laughed out loud. "How do you not?"

Her parents were correct. The dude was a loon. "That's not even funny."

"He's just outside. Right down the street. On his knees from the pain of losing you for the entire world to see. If you hurry, you can catch him before the sun rises and the humans wake up to chase him away. For then, it will be too late."

When she didn't move, he stood up and grabbed her by the arm to lift her to her feet. "Go! Go! We can talk more later."

Heather winced as he gave her an overly enthusiastic push toward the door, uncaring of her remaining injuries that hadn't quite healed yet. "All right! All right. I'm going. Jeez." Taking him up on this opportunity to get the hell out of there, she limped as fast as she could go to the front door and let herself out.

Stepping out onto the small porch, she hobbled down the steps and stopped to get her bearings. A light, misty rain was falling, and she took a deep breath of the fragrant air. She would be sad later, when she was home. She would cry, and eat ice cream, and watch bad T.V. once she reached the comfort of her own couch. Right now, she was running on autopilot.

Glancing to her left, she squinted in the darkness, trying to decide on the quickest way to a phone. After the brightness of the kitchen, she could barely see anything. She briefly thought about going back in to see if His Craziness had one he would let her use, but decided she would rather hobble all the way back to the airport and find a phone there.

As her eyes adjusted, she thought she remembered coming in from her right, so she turned in that direction. She hadn't gone three uneven steps when she stopped short. There, in the middle of the road about a hundred yards away, was a giant heap of something large and dark.

It was Brock. On his knees. Just down the street.

CHAPTER 21

Brock took a shuddering breath and sat up, wiping his face and pushing his hair back off of his forehead with both hands. He needed to move. To go. To get the fuck away from this house and this road and these crazy creatures. He needed to go home, and get back to his normal, lonely life. Everything would be all right once he got home. Things would go back to the way they were and this week and everything that had happened would fade day by day until eventually, it would be nothing but a vague memory.

And he was full of shit.

He was a werewolf. And werewolves fell hard when they met their female. And they only loved once. And he would *never* forget.

The hair rose on the back of his neck. He was being watched. Without giving away the fact that he knew, he forcibly pulled himself out of the bowels of the emotional hell he now found himself in and tuned in to what his senses were telling him.

Heather.

His heart flipped over in his chest. He didn't have to look to know it was her. He could smell her sultry fragrance; that light scent of heather blossoms and woman. He could fucking *feel* her there. His pulse sped up in excitement. She'd followed him outside. Why?

But he immediately squashed down any and all hope. *Or, maybe I've just been out here so damn long she was leaving to go back to her friend's.* And here he was, on his knees in the middle of the road like a goddamn pussy. As if he needed her feeling sorry for him on top of everything else.

Lumbering to his feet, he started to walk away without a backward glance, his face burning with embarrassment.

"Brock. Wait! Please."

Her voice flowed over his wounded soul, but he kept walking. He didn't want to hear how much he had hurt her. He knew. And he'd already apologized. There was nothing else to say.

"Brock, please. Help me out here," she called a little louder this time. "Ow."

He remembered her injuries, and with an inward curse he stopped. Clenching his fists at his sides, he turned back to see her limping after him as fast as she could go. She stumbled, crying out when she caught herself on her injured leg.

Without another thought for himself or his wounded ego, he rushed over and swooped her up into his arms. "What are ye doin'?" he growled. "Yer going tae injure yourself even worse."

Wrapping her arms around his neck and grinning up at him she said, "I know. I think you need to carry me."

So, that was her game. Slowly, reluctantly, he lowered her back down and steadied her until she was standing on her own two feet. "Heather, what are you doing?"

"Does this mean you're not going to carry me?" she asked. She looked so disappointed that he almost picked her back up again. Then she sighed. "It's okay. I know I'm a bit more than an armful."

He frowned down at her. "What are you blathering on about?"

She chewed on her bottom lip. She rubbed her palms on her thighs. She tried to untangle her hair.

"Heather. Why are you out here? Can I help you get a cab or something?"

She raised a brow. "Do you think they'll take those golden coins we've been collecting?"

Money. Right. They had none. "Can I help you get back to Grace's or wherever it is you were going?"

"Do you love me?" she blurted out. Then she slapped her hand over her mouth.

Gently, he pulled it away from her face and held it in between both of his. "I dae. Verra, verra much." His eyes were suspiciously moist, and he wiped the back of one hand over them.

"Then why are you leaving me?" she whispered.

Flabbergasted, he searched her pretty face. "I thought I should...I thought that was what you would want. You looked so upset with me..."

"Did you love her?" she interrupted. "I mean, you must have. She's...perfect."

He shook his head. "No. I didn't. I don't!" he scoffed. "And she is nowhere near 'perfect'. Not to me." He bent down until he was on a level with her to make sure she was paying close attention. "Heather, I was never with that woman."

"What do you mean?"

"It wasn't me." Would she believe him?

She wrinkled up her forehead. "But, I thought…you confessed…"

"Aye. I did. But I didn't do it. I was trying to protect… somebody." For some reason, he couldn't bring himself to say the bastard's name. "I was going to tell the truth, today. I was," he insisted. "I was going to tell everyone! But then Sara showed up with the child. And I just couldn't do it. I realized that if I told the truth now, I wouldn't be freeing myself, or getting back at the one who'd done it. I'd be condemning a female and her innocent child." He shrugged. "I just couldn't do that."

"Oh," she said. "But why were you going to tell the truth now? After all this time? After all you've been through?"

"Because I want to be with you. I want to be worthy of you." He sighed heavily. "I don't expect you to believe me…"

"I believe you."

"You do?" he asked in disbelief.

"I do. But it wouldn't have mattered anyway. Whatever happened or didn't happen is in the past. It has nothing to do with who you are now." She gave him a timid smile. "That's what I came out here to tell you."

He knew he loved this woman. She *had* come out here

after him before she even knew the truth of the matter. And that said a lot to him.

She backed away a few steps. "But, you know, if you've changed your mind now that we're back in reality, I totally get it. It's okay." She smiled, even though it looked like it pained her to do so. "I mean, it was crazy in there. And things happened. And it's totally cool. I don't expect you to marry me or anything."

"Heather."

"I mean, being sucked into another world like that…"

"Heather."

"That would mess with anyone's head."

He rested his hands on his narrow hips and cocked a brow at her. "Are you finished?"

She appeared to think about it for a few seconds. "Yes? Yes. I'm done."

Stepping closer to her, he tilted her face up to his and kissed her soundly on those beautiful lips. "Good," he breathed when he came up for air. "Because I want to stop talking now and take you somewhere where we can be alone and I can show you exactly how much I meant every single thing I've said the last few days."

Her eyes were large in her pretty face as she stared up at him. "Oh, okay."

"And I think I should carry you. Because I want to hold you."

"Okay," she breathed.

He smiled down at her. "Okay."

Scooping her effortlessly into his arms, he strode over to the truck he'd borrowed and deposited her inside of it.

"Where did you get this truck?" she asked once he'd joined her inside.

"I stole it so I could follow you here."

"Good call," she told him. "Where to now?"

The truck started with a rumble and he reached over to take her hand. "I thought we'd drop by Cedric's, the pack leader that was here earlier. Maybe he knows somewhere we can stay until we get our bearings again." He glanced over at her. "That is, if he doesn't demand I leave his territory as soon as he sets eyes on me again. I doubt all of this made a very impression."

"He won't," she told him.

"How do you know?"

"Just drive. I'll tell you about it on the way."

* * *

AS IT TURNED OUT, Cedric and Lucian were "having a blether" when they arrived at his place. He happily handed Brock a spare credit card with the directions to use it for whatever they needed, and gave him directions to the nearest hotel. He also gave him the keys to a legal vehicle and promised to have one of the "pups" take care of the borrowed truck as soon as he was done "getting th' truth out o' this eejit", casually pointing his thumb back to where Lucian was perched on the edge of his sofa. Standing in front of him were two more males, both with arms crossed over their chests. The one with short, dark hair didn't look surprised to be in this situation. The other one glanced up and gave Heather a saucy wink, then grinned at Brock when he growled quietly at him.

"I still believe yer a braw lad, Brock," Cedric told him as they were leaving. "And I would like to hear yer side of things, and maybe discuss your future. Why dinna you and yer lass come back here for dinner the day after tomorrow?"

"I would appreciate the chance to do that. Thank you," Brock told him, his voice full of respect.

"Och. Aye. Go on wit' ye now. I'll see you both in a couple of days." And then he closed the door in their face.

The hotel was only a few blocks away, and Brock quickly secured a room and hurried Heather into it. He'd barely closed the door behind them before he grabbed her and backed her up against the wall. Planting a hand on either side of her so she couldn't escape, he gave her one last chance to change her mind. "Are you very sure about this, sunshine? I don't know what's going to happen from here on out, or where I'm going to end up, or what I'll be doing."

Planting her hands firmly on his hard chest, she peeked up at him from under her lashes. "I want to be with you," she stated. "But there are some things you should know first."

Warmth and desire rippled through him at her words, so much so he barely heard the second part of what she'd said. Burying his face in the side of her neck, he mumbled, "What things?"

"Brock, listen."

Reluctantly, he lifted his head and gave her his attention.

"Prince Nada told me some things. He said..."

"Nada? His name is Nada?" He barked out a laugh. She rolled her eyes and he got serious again. "Sorry. Go on."

"So, you know that place that the bad Fae were banished to? The one I was telling you about?"

He nodded.

"Well, it's going to open again. And they're going to get out. The prince is worried, and I believe he's sincere."

"What's that got to do with us?" he asked, his eyes straying to the firm roundness of the tops of her full breasts. As if they felt his eyes on them, her nipples strained against the fabric of her tee shirt, begging for his attention. And boy, did they have it. His cock responded eagerly, pushing against the confines of his pants. Lowering his hand from the wall, he cupped the weight of one soft mound, running his thumb over the hard nub at the tip.

Heather caught her breath. "You're distracting me."

"Am I?" He pinched her nipple between his thumb and forefinger, and she moaned. "Ye better hurry up and finish telling me then, because I cannae wait much longer to have you, sunshine." Lowering his other hand, he gripped her hip to hold her still while he continued to tease her.

"Um," she murmured, her eyes closing. "They're getting out. And he wanted us to hook up so you could talk other wolves into helping us contain them again." Her hands slid down his sides to his waist, where they found they're way under his shirt. "Or to kill them. Whatever works."

Gripping the bottom of her shirt, he yanked it up over her head. "Anything for you, sunshine. Anything." Lowering his head, he captured her lips with his.

Thrusting his tongue inside, he ravaged her sweet mouth until she was moaning and breathless.

Her palms pressed against his bare chest, and she broke off the kiss. "I need a shower," she protested as he yanked her bra down under her breasts.

Kissing his way from her mouth to her ear and down her neck, his hand found its way around to her luscious ass. He yanked her up against his hardness, lifting her and rolling his hips against her. "Do ye want me tae stop?"

"God, no. I was just warning you," she answered.

With a low growl, he yanked her pants down, ripping them off when they got stuck around her makeshift splint. Undoing his pants, he released his engorged shaft with a hiss. Stepping into Heather again, he slid both hand under her ass and lifted her against the wall.

She wrapped her good leg around his waist, opening herself to him and he positioned himself at her entrance. A brief moment of sanity hit him. "Are you ready for me, sunshine? I dinna want to hurt you."

Wiggling her hips, she rubbed herself against the tip of his cock. She was damp and warm, and he twitched in response. "Yes. Brock. Please, fuck me," she moaned. "I need to feel you inside of me."

With a snarl, he thrust upward, impaling her to the hilt. "Ah! Gods..." She was tight and wet, her muscles squeezing him as he withdrew, only to sink deep inside of her again.

Her fingers gripped his shoulders and she leaned back against the wall, angling herself against him. With her thighs, she gripped his waist and began to rock against him.

He let her set the pace, grinding his jaw as he watched her move. Lowering his head, he sucked a nipple into his mouth. His tongue teased and she quickened her pace, crying out when he nipped her with his teeth. He felt the heaviness of his impending release tightening his balls, and released her nipple.

"Heather, I'm going to come," he panted. Gripping her ass hard, he took over, speeding up the pace and slamming her up and down until she cried out and threw her head back against the wall. With a roar, he joined her, emptying almost violently inside of her as she convulsed around him.

When he could breathe again, he wrapped her in his arms without pulling out of her. "Are you all right? I didn't mean to be so rough."

She kissed him on the cheek, nuzzling his short beard. "I heal quite fast," she pointed out. "Does this mean you're going to stay with me?"

Running one hand up her back again, he twisted his fingers into her hair and pulled her head back so he could look at her. "Just try tae get rid of me."

She smiled. "Your accent is sexy."

He frowned. "I worked hard to get rid of it, but it does tend to come out when I'm upset."

"Or overcome with lust for me?" She grinned up at him impishly.

"Och. Aye, sunshine." He kissed her again.

As she moaned in his arms, he strode into the bathroom to run that shower.

* * *

Thank you for reading! I hope you loved meeting Brock and Heather. The next book in The Kincaid Werewolves series is
A Wolf's Honor.
Marc travels to Texas to meet up with the local pack, which is dangerous enough for a shifter, only to find out the local entertainment is not your traditional rodeo, but one that has a sadistic twist. He has to choose between upholding the honor of his pack, or putting his life on the line to help a Fae lass save her family.

Author Note: Bronaugh Lane is one of my favorite heroines of this entire series. :D

CLICK HERE TO READ A WOLF'S HONOR NOW

"I always love the twists that Wilson gives to her world. She makes your classic shifter tale take such a unique turn..." - The Book Disciple Blog
"I love how Wilson writes her books. I love that there's so much happening. I never want to put the book down. I can't wait for the next one!" -Amazon review

Or keep reading for a sneak peak!

This is no' goin' tae end well.

Marc Kincaid rose to his impressive height from the park bench he'd been lounging on. He eyed the threesome of sizable Lycan males sauntering toward him at typical southern speed across the front lawn of the Texas Capitol building. He sighed heavily, and wished they would hurry it the fuck up.

He silently reviewed what he was planning to say to them, calculated the risks of saying this and not saying that, and prayed the hellish heat didn't make them ill-tempered. He just needed them to listen for a few minutes. But even from this distance, one look at their stony faces and he was more certain than ever that this was naught but a mistake. He was wasting his time.

But it was what his alpha wanted, and he'd agreed to try. Cedric hadn't been pack leader for this long without knowing what he was doing.

As they neared, Marc's eyebrow rose at their wannabe

cowboy ensembles: button-down shirts with rolled up sleeves, well-worn jeans, cowboy boots, and large brimmed hats slung down low on their foreheads. He half expected to hear jangling spurs and see stalks of hay sticking out from between their teeth, and was almost disappointed when he didn't. He couldn't quite keep the smirk from his face as he wondered if they all gathered round the campfire every night and planned what they were going to wear the next morning so they would all match.

They even had giant silver buckles on their belts, even though Marc knew for a fact that not a one of them had ever ridden a bull. Bucking chute or not, there was no way an animal would allow any of their kind to get close enough to be able to climb onto its back. The poor thing would break its wee neck trying to escape first.

Arms hanging at his sides in a deceptively relaxed pose, Marc discreetly cracked his knuckles one by one, then wiped his sweaty palms on his jean-clad thighs. He wasn't nervous. Quite the opposite, actually. His wolf was well under control, which was how he liked it, and this meeting was taking place on neutral ground in full view of the humans milling about on their lunch hour. Unless these guys were a special kind of eejit, there wouldn't be any violence here today. He was only sweating because it was unbelievably hot in Austin, even this late in the summer. He didn't know how anyone could live here, be they human or otherwise, and especially not a pack of werewolves. Like him, their body temperature ran a little hotter than what was normal, and they were definitely better suited for a cooler climate. Why in all that was holy would these fools choose to live here?

He eyeballed their ridiculous ensembles once more and sighed.

Well, at least they seem tae have adapted well tae the local urban cowboy culture.

A slight breeze blew through the scrub brush Texans called trees and Marc squinted against the dust. Even the bloody wind was hot here. He squinted up at the scorching sun. He was beginning to see why everyone moved at a snail's pace here. Scratching the back of his neck, he contemplated sitting down again as it seemed he was going to be waiting a while. It was bad etiquette as he'd already stood to greet them, but fuck it. If they couldn't get their arses over to him in a proper amount of time, then he saw no need to act any differently.

The wind changed course, blowing in from the opposite direction, and he stopped mid-sit. Marc shot upright again, inhaling deeply. His entire body went rigid, straining in the direction of a new, intriguing scent. Digging his utility boots into the grass, he fought the urge to charge off after it with his nose lifted in the air like a hound.

What the hell is that?

It seemed vaguely familiar to him, but wasn't anything he could immediately place his finger on. Yet it called to him with such a force that he was having a bloody hard time resisting.

What the fook is that?

After racking his brain for a full minute, it finally came to him, the place he'd smelled it before. It was Northern

Ireland. Or rather, a brief moment of time he'd spent in Ireland a long, long time ago.

Many moons before, his pack had crossed the North Channel from their homeland of Scotland after rumors of Faerie problems had made it to their ears. He'd been in his wolf form, standing alone in an open field and trying to catch his breath after he'd just run full-out for many miles. Panting heavily, he'd lifted his snout to the sky and breathed in the strong smells of the grass and the wildflowers, made musky from the recent rain. But there'd been one scent that had seemed to overpower all of the others: the heady fragrance of what he'd later discovered had come from the creamy-white meadowsweet flowers.

Those flowers were native to Ireland, however, so how was it that he was smelling them here? All the way across the ocean? In the desert landscape of Texas, of all places?

His narrowed gaze swept across the manicured lawn of the capitol building. He searched the flowerbeds, the bushes, the trees...but saw nothing that even slightly resembled the dense white clusters he was accustomed to seeing. And then, just as quickly as it had appeared, the smell was gone. Immediately, his muscles relaxed, his heart slowed, and his attention once again turned to the approaching pack of werewolves who were suddenly uncomfortably close to him.

Shaking off the strange occurrence, he kept his gaze steady but passive on the leader of the pack, careful to emit neither dominance nor submissiveness. He wasn't here to have a pissing contest, but rather to warn them of the war that was coming and to propose an alliance between their two packs. There was only one other pack that had taken up residence in the land between them on this side of the North American continent, for werewolf territory ranged far and wide. And if Marc could get these Texas wolves to agree to the truce, it would be easier to talk the middle pack into falling in with them.

The male in front came to a stop a respectable distance away and touched the brim of his buckskin-colored hat. Clear green eyes shone from tanned skin at a level with Marc's own. "Afternoon," he drawled. "Marc Kincaid, I take it?"

Marc gave him a nod of deference as befitted the leader of a rival pack. "Aye. Thank ye for agreeing tae meet me on such short notice, and under these circumstances. Cedric sends his apologies that he could no' make it himself. He had an urgent matter tae attend tae." Marc had no idea exactly what the "urgent matter" was. And when he'd asked, Cedric had danced around the subject until he'd given up.

The alpha nodded once, accepting the apology. "I'm Keegan. Alpha of the McRae pack here." He nodded to the pale-skinned blond on his right. "This is Jace, my second-in-command."

Jace crossed his arms over his muscular chest and gave Marc an arrogant stare, his blue eyes narrowed with mistrust. His cocky attitude reminded Marc of Lucian, and he struggled not to snarl back at him. He didn't like this one. Not one bit.

"And this," Keegan indicated the male to his left, "is Stone."

Marc didn't even bother to try to hide his surprise as Stone stuck out his hand with a wide smile of welcome.

"I'm a bit of a surprise to new people, I know. But here I am," he told Marc amiably. "Welcome to Texas."

"Uh, thank ye," Marc mumbled automatically as he took the proffered hand and gave it a firm shake. He briefly studied the warm umber skin, dark eyes, and broad features before his gaze came to rest on the fangs that were glaringly obvious by that friendly grin. "I apologize for starin'," he said after a long moment. "It's just a wee bit o' a surprise tae meet a male such as yerself."

Although Stone's scent was overpoweringly wolf, there was a tinge of something "other" there as well. If Marc wasn't mistaken, he was staring at the first werewolf half-breed he'd ever met. Or had ever even heard of, for that matter. But it wasn't vampire. He knew the scent of vampires. As a matter of fact, some of his very good friends back home in Seattle were vamps. No. This was something else. These American wolves were just full of surprises.

But Stone just gave a deep chuckle and clapped him on the shoulder. "I understand, man. No worries. No worries. I get that a lot."

Marc waited for him to say more, but it seemed there was to be no further explanation forthcoming. He didn't know what else had sired this male, but whatever it was, it was powerful. That much he could sense.

"Stone is relatively new to our pack, but as you can well imagine, he's turned out to be quite an asset," Keegan told him.

Marc glanced uneasily one more time at those ominous fangs that were such a contrast to the carefree grin that encased them, and then turned his attention back to the pack leader. "However do ye manage to keep him under yer thumb?"

Keegan laughed and gave a small shrug with one powerful shoulder. "My charming personality?" Stone busted up laughing.

Cracking a smile, Marc decided that he liked this particular Texan, in spite of his silly clothes and accent.

"How about we wander over to The Chili Parlor and have us a sit-down?" Keegan said. "Then you can tell us what's so damn important that it brings you all the way down here from Seattle."

Marc didn't know what a "chili parlor" was, but if it involved food, he was all for it. He was starving. So he agreed without hesitation. "Sounds like a fine plan."

There was little talking as they made their way over to The Chili Parlor, which turned out to be a little restaurant that served what was reputed to be some of the best chili in Texas. Making their way over to an empty booth, Marc observed Jace elbowing Stone out of the way to take his place by Keegan's side. Stone rolled his eyes and slid in the other side, leaving Marc the spot on the end. Granting him an easy escape if need be.

His trust in this pack grew a little bit more.

They ordered lunch and as they waited for their food, Keegan put his elbows on the table and laced his fingers together. He was suddenly all business.

Taking his cue, Marc mimicked his pose.

"So now, why don't you tell me what this visit is all about," Keegan said. "It's not often we receive a request for a sit-down from a rival pack. If this were a normal challenge for territory or females, we would just fight it out in the traditional way. And the fact that we're not tells me that this has nothing to do with either of those. Am I right?"

"Aye," Marc agreed. "Ye are correct. This is much more serious than either o' those." Three pairs of eyes were on him now.

Keegan sat back as the food arrived. Smiling at the waitress, he waited for her to leave before he picked up the conversation again. It took her a while, but when she could think of nothing else to offer them without being so blatantly obvious that it would get her fired, she finally gave them another pile of napkins and went to check her other tables.

Picking up his spoon, Keegan said, "Well, might as well lay it on me." Then he dug into his chili with such relish Marc wondered what it was exactly that was in this chili.

"Aye." Marc paused, running his well-rehearsed words through his mind. But in the end, he decided there was no sense in beating around the bush. "They're comin'."

"Who?" Jace asked with an impatient tone.

"The soul suckers." Marc took a big bite of his chili and moaned with approval. He took another bite, and another. They were right. This was some bloody good chili. With his fourth spoonful halfway to his mouth, he realized the rest of the table wasn't eating anymore.

They were staring at him in horror.

Bronaugh watched the four werewolves eat their chili from her perch on the small retaining wall across the street. A sudden sharp pain on her finger distracted her from her vigil, and she looked down at her hand to see a fire ant chomping away on her knuckle.

She flicked it off with a curse. Gods, she hated Texas. Everything here either bit you or stung you. And you didn't have to be visible for them to find you either; the damn things sniffed you out from a mile away. Ignoring the sweat trickling down her spine, she went back to spying on the werewolves.

Uh oh. Something big was going down. She could tell by the look on the alpha's face as he spoke to the blond. And by the harsh lines twisting his handsome features, it wasn't good.

Leaning forward, she tucked her hair behind one slightly pointed ear and strained to hear what was happening. But it was no use. Between the traffic, the glass window, and the chattering humans as they bustled around on their lunch hour, she couldn't hear a word of what the wolves were saying. But she didn't dare try to get closer again. That damn new wolf had nearly sniffed her out back at the capitol the last time she'd tried that. With an impatient sigh, she leaned back on her hands again and continued to watch and observe. After all, that was what she did best.

What she really wanted to know was: who was the new guy? And what was he doing with these dickwads? She'd been trailing this pack for months now, and this was the first time she'd seen *that* particular tower of hunkiness. She was sure of it. A male like that she would've remembered. There was no doubt about it. Even now, her eyes continued to be drawn back to him again and again, instead of concentrating on trying to read the pack leader's lips.

When she'd first seen the new guy waiting on the others in front of the capitol, her stomach had given a lurch and chills had shot down her arms—and not in a bad way. That canine was one manly hunk of wolf. And she would've bet anyone a shitload of money that he smelled great too. With her blood roaring through her veins loud enough to drown out the warning her brain had been trying to tell her, she'd been unable to resist. She had to see him up close and personal. Stepping heel to toe so as not to make the slightest sound, she'd walked right up to him while praying to any gods that happened to be listening that he wouldn't hear the pounding of her heart. She'd snuck so close, in fact, that she'd been able to see the depths of color in his eyes—such a deep brown they were nearly black, but with little tiny gold flecks in them. Darker than her own orbs. Darker than his hair that fell in short layers just to the bottom of his strong, tanned neck. She'd hoped to get near enough to be able to hear his voice. But then he'd suddenly straightened to his imposing height, and his powerful body had tensed as those sharp eyes studied his surroundings with new interest. Knowing she'd been sensed, she'd panicked and quickly retreated to a safe distance and then some.

Bronaugh sighed. She supposed it would all be revealed in time.

Maybe he was here hoping to get into their pack, although he didn't seem to act like a young pup who was trying to win over the alpha. He appeared respectful to the pack leader, yes, but not overly so. He certainly wasn't groveling. Was he an alpha from a different pack? But that didn't make sense either. Rival pack leaders didn't sit around and talk through their differences over lunch. They settled things the way wolves always did. Physically. And may the more dominant and powerful male or female win.

The blond said something to the new guy, but the way his head was turned, she couldn't quite make out what he was saying. Whatever it was blondie was saying, he wasn't happy about it. Then again, that dude didn't seem to like it when anyone took the spotlight away from him. The alpha spoke to him, and Bronaugh could practically hear the patronizing tone in his voice from all the way across the street. But then he threw his hands up in the air and let the blond out of the booth. With one last parting shot she lip-read to be something like "Y'all are a bunch of morons," he stomped out of the restaurant and took off down the street.

And the plot thickened.

She debated whether or not to follow him, but decided to stay where she was. For although she was pretty sure the blond was the key to finding what she was looking for, she couldn't seem to force herself away from the stranger who even now was staring right at her through the window.

Wait. He was staring right at her!

Bronaugh froze, unsure what to do. Even with the street and sidewalks of people between them, his eyes bore right through to shake her very core. Without taking his eyes from her, he said something to the others at the table. The alpha and the dark-skinned one both started searching the people lingering outside the restaurant. Then the alpha shrugged. He said something to the new guy, who blinked and turned to glance at him. As soon as he took his eyes away from her, she made herself scarce.

Running as fast as she could, she headed toward the UT campus. She needed people to hide among. It was summer, so it wouldn't be as crowded as normal there, but she didn't know where else to go. She could only hope he didn't take her disappearing act as a challenge and give chase.

CHAPTER 3

Marc busted out of the restaurant and searched the area. Careful not to knock down any pedestrians, he made his way to the outer edge of the sidewalk and looked up and down the street.

He could've sworn he'd seen something, or someone, watching them from the wall on the other side.

"Don't worry, lunch is on me," Keegan joked as he and Stone joined him outside.

Marc shook himself for the second time that day. "Did ye see something? Across the road there?" He pointed at the stone wall that bordered the small slope of lawn.

"Something like what, exactly?" Stone asked.

"I thought I saw a lass…" Looking around again, Marc shook his head. "Never mind. It was nothin'. I think the heat is making me daft."

Keegan glanced around. "I didn't see anything, man. But maybe you should drink some water. Sounds like you're dehydrated."

"It's verra possible."

Glancing around one more time, Keegan took off his hat and scratched his head before covering his short dark hair again. "I'm sure it was nothing. Humans stare at us a lot."

"And who can blame them? Especially the females," Stone added with another grin, careful to keep his fangs under wraps around the humans who were milling about waiting for their tables.

"Ach. Aye. You're right. It was probably nothin'," Marc acceded. Yet he still had the strangest feeling it wasn't nothing. That it was actually a very big something.

"Tell you what," Keegan told him. "We have to head out. I've got another appointment I need to get to and I need Stone with me for this one." He took off his hat and wiped the sweat from his brow, then looked up rather sheepishly. "Honestly, I didn't expect this 'meeting' to happen. I was half expecting to get jumped. But why don't you come by the house tomorrow afternoon and we can talk some more? If what you were saying is true, we have some more things to discuss. Do you have a cell on you? I'll give you the address."

Marc pulled out his phone and saved the address Keegan gave him.

"If Jace was still here, I'd have him show you around a bit…"

"That's quite okay," Marc assured him. "I have a map." He pulled one out of his pocket that he'd picked up when he'd hit Austin. "I can find my way."

They shook hands and the cowboys took off, leaving Marc alone on the street. He watched them until they turned the corner, then he looked both ways before dodging four lanes of traffic to the other side of the street.

It wasn't "nothing." He'd seen someone watching them. He was sure of it. Listening to his instincts, he headed in the opposite direction, toward the college. He'd only gone about three blocks when he caught his first whiff.

Meadowsweet flowers after a heavy rain.

As the scent hit his nostrils for the second time that day, his entire body shot awake almost violently, and he allowed himself to do what he'd wanted to do back at the capitol. Letting his nose guide him, he hung a sharp left and then a right onto Guadalupe, dodging humans and moving as casually as he could. He followed the scent a few more blocks before coming to an abrupt stop in the middle of the sidewalk.

Dammit. He'd lost it.

Glancing around, he saw he was in front of the University Co-op. He pulled open the door and was immediately assaulted with racks and racks of burnt orange—T-shirts, sweatshirts, hats, backpacks—anything a burgeoning UT college student could ever need to support his or her school team.

And meadowsweet after the rain.

"Can I help you find anything?" The question came out a bit breathless.

Marc barely glanced at the young female who apparently worked there. "Nae. I'm good, thank ye." She blinked hard a few times at what he could only assume was the accent, smiled a strange smile, opened her mouth to say something, but then turned abruptly and went back to the clothes she was in the process of hanging on the wall display. Every few seconds, she would glance at him out of the corner of her eye and smile as a blush reddened her cheeks.

Marc cocked an eyebrow. The cowboys may have had a point about the females flirting with them here. In Seattle, they weren't quite so transparent about it, if they swooned over him at all. Of course, it rained a lot there. And most everyone went about their business under the cover of raincoats, with their noses in their coffees.

Turning his back to her, he surveyed the store, searching for…he didn't know who, or what. He followed the scent to a back clothing rack with a big "Clearance" sign on it and pretended to look for something in his size as he made his way around the circle of clothing. The musky smell got stronger as he got closer to the rear corner of the store. It flooded his senses until he could barely think, but try as he might, he couldn't pinpoint where it was coming from. And he even checked inside the clothing racks.

With a frown he pulled his head out of the clothes to see the salesgirl watching him from a few racks away, and she wasn't smiling this time. Rather she looked like she was wondering if she needed to call for backup.

"Are you sure I can't help you find something?" she asked warily.

With a start, he realized he'd been looking through the women's section. Marc forced himself to smile at her. "Cannae find a shirt large enough to fit me."

"The *men's* big and tall section is over there," she told him, indicating the other side of the store.

"Ach. Aye. Thank ye." Not knowing what else to do

without making himself look even more suspicious, he headed over that way and proceeded to look for something in his size. The intriguing scent of the flowers faded as he walked away. But he didn't know what else he could do without raising more suspicion, and that he could not do. Staying under the radar of the humans was fundamental to their survival.

* * *

BRONAUGH HELD her breath as she watched the werewolf move away from her and head to the other side of the store. As soon as he was far enough away, she blew out a relieved breath. Then as quietly as she could, she made her way back toward the front doors and waited until another customer came in. A young guy flung open the door after just a few seconds and blew inside, and Bronaugh ducked under his arm and rushed past him and out of the store before it closed again.

Running full-out, she put as much distance as she could between herself and that male. She didn't bother cloaking her form anymore—she was moving too fast for the human eye to track now anyway. No one would see her until she stopped, and she wasn't stopping until she got to her room at the Holiday Inn.

When she got to First Street, she hit the hike-and-bike trail that hugged the edge of Lady Bird Lake and dropped down into the water, disguising her trail with the smell of fish and algae. She wasn't taking any chances that the wolf would follow her to her only safe place here. Back up on the trail, she blasted past the joggers, not slowing until she got to her hotel near I-35. Dodging a group of runners, she took the path that connected the trail and the hotel and walked into the foyer. The hot Texas sun had nearly dried her clothes already, so she didn't attract any undue attention as she got into the elevator. Letting herself into her room, she locked the door and leaned back against it.

Breathe, Bronaugh. Just breathe.

That had been entirely too close. How could she have been so stupid? She'd almost let herself be seen by the creatures that had been hunting her and her kind for hundreds of years. Getting herself captured now was not going to help her family. And now that she'd tracked them to this city, she needed to keep her wits about her so they didn't slip out of her grasp again.

She knew those wolves had something to do with her family's disappearance. Tomorrow, she was going to follow the new guy and find out for herself.

And when she showed herself, it would be on her terms. Not his.

CLICK HERE TO READ A WOLF'S HONOR NOW

THE
KINCAID
WEREWOLVES
BOOK TWO
A Wolf's
Honor
L. E. WILSON

L.E. Wilson writes Paranormal Romance starring intense alpha males and the women who are fearless enough to tame them — for the most part anyway. ;) In her novels you'll find smoking hot scenes, a touch of suspense, some humor, a bit of gore, and multifaceted characters, all working together to combine her lifelong obsession with the paranormal and her love of romance.

Her writing career came about the usual way: on a dare from her loving husband. Little did she know just one casual suggestion would open a box of worms (or words as the case may be) that would forever change her life.

Peach tea and her tiara are a necessary part of her writing process, though sometimes you'll find her typing away at her favorite Starbucks. She walks two miles to get there, to make up for all of those coffees. On the weekends she likes to hike, garden, cook vegan food, and have date nights with her favorite guy.

On a Personal Note:
"I love to hear from my readers! Contact me anytime at le@lewilsonauthor.com."

Keep In Touch With L.E.
lewilsonauthor.com
le@lewilsonauthor.com